THE FINAL
GAUNTLET

Also by Lou Paduano

The Greystone Saga

Signs of Portents
Tales from Portents
The Medusa Coin
Pathways in the Dark
A Circle of Shadows

Greystone-in-Training

Hammer and Anvil
The Gifts of Kali

The DSA

Season One

The Clearing
Promethean
The Bridge
Spectral Advocate
Dark Impulses
Broken Loyalties

THE FINAL
GAUNTLET

Greystone-in-Training Book Three

Lou Paduano

Eleven Ten Publishing LLC

GRAND ISLAND, NEW YORK

Eleven Ten Publishing LLC
282 Fareway Lane
Grand Island, NY 14072

Publisher's note: This is a work of fiction. Names, characters, places, and
incidents either are the product of the author's imagination or are used
fictitiously. Any resemblance to actual events, locales, or persons, living or
dead, is entirely coincidental.

Printed in the United States of America
Edited by JD Book Services
Cover art design by MiblArt

First edition published 2020

Library of Congress Cataloguing in Publication Data
Paduano, Lou
The Final Gauntlet / Lou Paduano

LCCN: 2020917206
ISBN-13: 978-1-944965-67-9 (hardcover)
ISBN-13: 978-1-944965-34-1 (paperback)
ISBN-13: 978-1-944965-33-4 (eBook)

To my family,
for helping me reach the finish line.

CHAPTER ONE

Soriya Greystone picked at a plate of home fries. Her scrambled eggs and toast had already been devoured. The diner had become one of Soriya's favorites when her friend had introduced her to the delicacies conjured in the kitchen. Whenever the opportunity came up to meet somewhere, it was Soriya's first choice. Bethany Loren had no complaints about the selection.

Another forkful of food slid between Soriya's lips. An eggy residue ran along her chin, and she swiped at it with her napkin. Beth sat across from her in the corner booth. She held a cup of coffee between her hands. Her gaze wandered outside at the slowly rising sun, distracted from the story Soriya shared.

"So I'm wrestling with this Yeren while his girlfriend is watching," Soriya said. She tried to keep her voice down to avoid the attention of the other patrons in the diner. Her excitement, however, made it difficult. "She's screaming. She thinks his transformation into a monster is a sign of their love. Like, lady, he was planning on eating you. Not that she would hear any of it. So we're wrestling, and I get my stone ready to char his ass—it's a thing—whatever. And do you know what he does?"

Beth remained silent. As the pause lingered, her attention returned from the window. She offered a slight shake of her head.

"He licks me," Soriya exclaimed. "He licks me!"

She laughed, brash and boisterous. Beth stayed silent. Her eyes continued to wander away from the table. Soriya popped a slice of bacon into her mouth and chewed. Bits flew to her plate as she continued.

"I damn near slugged his face off I was so angry. Licked me!" She waited for a reaction. None came. Beth merely toyed with the handle of her coffee cup. "Grossest thing ever. So I take him out with the stone. Bye-bye, sicko. Then his girlfriend starts. She's jealous over the whole thing! Doesn't even realize he's not coming back. She's so focused on the wet one he planted on my cheek."

Soriya took another bite of bacon. Settling in her seat, she rested her arm along the back and turned to rest against the window frame.

"People are crazy," Soriya muttered. Her smile faded at the distant look in her companion's eyes. "Right, Beth?"

The young woman, one of Soriya's closest and most trusted associates, was lost to the sunrise and the city outside.

Soriya shifted away from the window, leaning closer to the table. "Beth?"

The name shook her from her thoughts and the blonde snapped back to the table. "Huh? Oh yeah. Crazy."

"What's wrong?"

"With me?" Beth replied. She waved off the question with a smile. "Pfft. Nothing. Not a thing. Why?"

Soriya saw through the act, more concerned than ever. "For one, you're not drinking your coffee."

"Stomach is off, that's all," her friend said.

"You sure?" Her hand fell on Beth's instead. "Hey. I'm here if you—"

Beth pulled away, her gaze focused on the table rather than meeting Soriya's eyes. "Just some work stuff. Don't worry about it."

Work stuff meant research. Beth was a historian; her focus was the city of Portents. It was how they'd met in the first place. Beth had been hunting down clues regarding the hammer of Hephaestus, as it related to a recent robbery. Soriya happened to be searching for an escaped minotaur at the time when they'd bumped into each other. Utilizing each other's specialized skill sets had brought them together and cemented their friendship.

Beth was one of the few people to understand the truth behind Portents. She saw the myths and legends of old that hid in the shadows and accepted them as part of the world. Knowing the truth about Portents empowered her. It didn't frighten her as it did so many others.

Portents meant everything to Beth. That and her husband, Greg. If something was bothering her, Soriya wanted to help. Beth, however, stayed silent on the subject.

Instead of pushing, Soriya let the moment fade. It wasn't her place to pry. She merely uttered a quiet, "Okay."

Beth offered a grateful nod, and she lifted her cup to her lips. Sharp blue eyes grew wide, and the cup returned to the table. "I almost forgot."

She scrounged around her purse and unzipped multiple pockets in order to find something. After digging through the contents, she exhaled a sigh of relief and removed the object from within. She passed it over to Soriya. "Here."

"What is it?" Soriya asked curiously. The box was wrapped in striped paper with a pink bow on top.

"An early graduation gift," Beth said. "I know the big test is coming up and you're nervous—even though you're going to do great."

The big test: Mentor's final challenge in order for her to officially become the Greystone. Soriya had been waiting weeks for it to happen, ever since he'd mentioned it during one of their late-night training sessions.

"Anyway," Beth continued. "I wanted you to have this."

Soriya tore through the wrapping. Pieces flew across the table until the packaging came into view. Soriya held the item between them, and her brow furrowed.

"A phone?"

Beth smiled. "So you can call me right after."

Soriya rested the gift on the table. "Beth."

"To celebrate, Soriya," Beth said. "It's a big deal. After Mentor's test, I... I know you'll be busy. Too busy for this."

"Never."

"People say that, Soriya." Beth's smile disappeared. "You might think of this as the end, as your last challenge to become the Greystone. But it's really only the start for you. Your world is going to get so much bigger, and with that comes change. It happens to everyone. The world moves on. With this, though, you can always reach me."

Soriya reached and took Beth's hand. She squeezed hard, unwilling to let her friend go. "You can call me too. You know that, right?"

"Absolutely."

Soriya nodded. Accepting the answer, she dropped Beth's hand. She was grateful for the gift. Soriya tucked the phone away, then relaxed against the soft cushion of the booth.

"So tell me about this work stuff."

"Soriya, I…" Beth's phone buzzed in her pocket. "Sorry." She pulled the small device out and read the message on the screen. With each word, creases formed along her brow and her shoulders slumped.

"What is it?" Soriya asked.

Beth put the phone away and immediately threw some cash on the table to cover the check. Then she shuffled for the end of the booth, gathering up her belongings as she went.

"I have to go." Beth stood and slung her purse over her shoulder. "Take care of yourself out there, okay?"

"I…" Soriya tried to find a way to stop her friend's departure. She fought for some reason to keep her in place and keep the conversation going. Beth's full attention, however, was on the front door of the diner. There was no keeping her there and no way to determine the cause of Beth's worry. Soriya could only mutter, "Yeah. You do the same."

Beth didn't bother to wait for the reply. She kept her eyes on the exit, never turning back to Soriya. Her quick steps carried her across the street and out of sight.

She wished Beth had offered her an explanation for what was bothering her. It wasn't like her friend to keep secrets. The silence spoke to the truth of the matter more than the woman was willing to admit. Soriya couldn't help but wonder what was wrong with her friend and why it concerned her so much.

CHAPTER TWO
One Month Later

It was time.

Annabelle Waterhouse knew it as soon as she woke up. The feeling ate at her like a cancer. It stirred her thoughts and drove her toward her goal. She tried to resist the urge as nothing more than the impetuousness of youth. She knew deep down, however, the time had come to try again.

Books lay in large piles on every counter in her cramped one-room apartment. Some were opened, and the texts within were littered with stray notes and circled objects. Lists marred the edges of each page. Some related to specific tasks to be completed, while others connected to different writings entirely.

The research had taken time, though it was something she skimped on in the beginning. That had proved to be a fatal flaw—the mistake that had followed all her attempts since. Even after months of preparation, Annabelle had jumped the gun last time. She had let excitement give way to arrogance, and another bitter failure was the result.

Not this time. Not again. Another mistake could not and would not occur again if it fell within her power. Days slipped to weeks, which turned to months, in her efforts to find the right tools for the job ahead.

She found rare ointments and elixirs. There were potions and brews lost to history, but she searched them out to gain access to their potency. Everything was in service of her goal. Fear held her back, but it could not stop her endless pursuit.

Annabelle shuffled her belongings into a knapsack. She delicately placed the items inside to avoid any unseemly collision of the volatile chemicals in each vial. She tucked the books in the back to keep the glass from shifting inside.

Placing the pack by the door, she reached for the coat rack and the lone cloak hanging from the hook. The cloak was long and trailed down to her knees when she slipped it on. The deep green cloth contained golden runic patterns along the back and sleeves. Annabelle tied it tight to her waist and let out a long breath.

She stopped in front of the mirror beside the door. She picked at stray locks of crimson hair to pull them away from her emerald eyes. Her lips were thin and her cheekbones were sunken against her gaunt figure. Who did they belong to? Which feature had been her father's? She wondered with each glance. Did her mother share her green eyes? Did her father carry the same wild hair? She knew nothing of them and nothing from her past.

Her every endeavor was to learn the truth about her origins. She had called the city outside home for as long she could remember, but Portents was not her true home. It held no family, no lineage, or legacy. Her childhood had been one of loneliness and desperation; she had sought out friendships and connections only to find emptiness in the attempts.

Annabelle Waterhouse didn't belong in Portents. She never had. Somewhere, though, was the truth. Tonight it was time to find out who she truly was and what she was meant for in the world.

The door would show her the way.

Twice now she had made the attempt. Both attempts had failed. This would be different. Her preparations had seen to that. Her dreams would make it a reality. All she required was a glimpse of the truth, a snapshot of her parents waiting for her on the other side ready to take her home.

It had to be tonight. Annabelle had spent so much time over the last year studying and researching. There was no more fear nor any doubts about what she had to do.

It was time to find her past and face her future.

Annabelle pulled the green hood over her head. It hid her scarlet hair and dropped her eyes into shadow. Her hand snatched up the knapsack, slipping the strap over her shoulder. Then she stepped out into the night, ready to face whatever lay ahead.

CHAPTER THREE

Life unfolded in the Courtyard. Soriya observed it all from the shadow of the alley. Across from her were the bronze entry doors to the hidden microcosm. She had been coming to this place since she was a child. Mentor had brought her to the Courtyard at an early age to see the wonders the true city held— and also so he could find a babysitter while he attended to a flock of harpies which sought revenge on a local gang.

There was always a new sight to see with each visit. Soriya stood in awe of the population residing within the twelve-block sanctuary. With doorways concealed throughout the space, the Courtyard bridged dozens of worlds and gave hundreds of unique creatures a place to call home. Thanks to the hidden space, they were allowed to live the way *they* chose rather than being pigeonholed into a certain role.

Elvish children rushed along the main road that cut through the space. They danced between the shoppers and the merchants, playing games and shouting laughter to anyone and everyone they met along the way. They ran recklessly, encircling the large right foot of a giant, who patted his stomach and muttered about the all-you-can-eat boar fest at the pavilion on the far end of the lane.

Laughter connected them all, from the street cart dealers to the residents in their mismatched homes. Some of the domiciles dated back decades, while others appeared as old as medieval times. The Courtyard transcended time and space. It pulled pieces of each era into its folds, while at the same time giving access to the multitude of worlds hidden just out of sight from the mundane and ignorant.

What it boiled down to was humanity. In that moment of pure relaxation, Soriya Greystone found the truest definition of humanity in watching the lives unfold around her. She realized the reason for her work, for every lesson learned and every task accomplished. It was for them and always would be. The thought made her proud.

She laughed, clapping along to the energetic, chaotic beat of the Courtyard. The sound filled the air, and her chest heaved from the pure joy in her heart.

The flapping of wings silenced her. Black and wide, they spread and gave flight to the raven called Kok'-Kol, who joined her at the mouth of the alley.

"It is good to hear you laugh, my child," the raven said.

"Kok'-Kol," Soriya said with a smirk. The raven landed on her shoulder. "I didn't think you were around. If I had known, I would have brought a treat."

Soriya left the street behind. The joy of the Courtyard fell into the background as the pair entered the darkness of the alley that served as the mighty raven's home. Kok'-Kol left the comfort of Soriya's shoulder and flew ahead. With each flap of his wings, torches flickered to life along the walls. The brick of tenement houses covered one side. The other was made up of cracked and broken stonework from the side of a castle. Kok'-Kol flew to the small altar at the back of the alley. He appeared to hover in the darkness.

"The thought is appreciated," Kok'-Kol replied. He lifted a wing and patted his gut. "I'm watching my figure anyway."

Soriya chuckled. "I'm sure."

"What brought about your visit tonight?"

"Well, I..." Soriya stopped when she realized the enjoyment behind the raven's question. She pointed to the winged beast. "You already know, don't you."

"I do."

Kok'-Kol was one the First Ones of the Miwok, an ancient tribe that, in their passing, became bound to their spirit animals. He had survived centuries as a raven thanks to his foresight—a gift that allowed him to view future events. It was in the sharing that he ran into trouble. Soriya had called him on it many times in the past, though she respected his methods and what he could offer to her.

"Mentor asked me to meet him here," Soriya explained. "I think he's planning his big test. He's going to pass on the role of Greystone finally."

Finally. Like it was a predetermined move by the man. Mentor wasn't that old. He still had plenty of years left where he could protect the city. Soriya understood that. She also knew that until he passed along the mantle, while others might call her Greystone, she would only ever be his student and nothing more. It was a role she'd grown frustrated with of late—like somewhere deep inside she knew it was time to move forward.

"*If* you succeed in this last trial," Kok'-Kol said.

"Thanks for the vote of confidence," Soriya said.

"I was merely reminding you to check your ego."

"I get it, Kok'-Kol."

"Do you now?" he replied, eyes piercing through the shadows. "I'm not so sure."

"Why? What have you seen?"

The raven hesitated. He dropped from the altar to a dumpster in the center of the alley. His beak picked at the remains on the small piece of cardboard covering the lid.

"It's not like you to hold back," Soriya said.

He caught the remark with a glare. Then he turned to face her. "Darkness and light I have seen. The door swings both ways. The daughters seek their kin to use for their own foul deeds. A choice will be made. Help her see the truth. She will be the key someday."

"But what—"

"You asked what I have seen, my child," Kok'-Kol interrupted. "That is what I have seen."

Soriya balled her hands into fists of frustration. "That doesn't explain anything though. You know that, right?"

"Next time you'll remember the treat, then, won't you?"

"Touché." Soriya huffed. She shook her head, and her hands fell open before clasping tight to her hips. "I'll be ready, Kok'-Kol."

The raven spread his wings to draw her in closer. Green eyes burned at her. "Do not listen to the voice, my child. It is from the past and the future. He will only lead you astray."

"What do you—"

Kok'-Kol took flight, which cut off her question. The black raven flew past Soriya for the open space of the Courtyard, rising higher and higher until he was gone.

"Thanks, Kok'-Kol," she muttered. His warning stayed with her. The raven, though stubborn in his insight, was never wrong. Kok'-Kol had never failed in his duty. His explanations simply took the long way around. One of these days she feared she might fail thanks to his games. She hoped it wasn't tonight. "What the hell did that mean?"

When her gaze fell back to earth, a shadow grew across the alley. A tall, lithe figure stood at the street, his tan cloak billowing in the breeze. Mentor's stern look was lost to the shadows, but his very presence made his intentions clear.

"Soriya." He held out his hand to her. "It's time."

CHAPTER FOUR

"You're kidding, aren't you?"

They had left the confines of the Courtyard in silence. It wasn't until they had reached the bottom of the steps that Mentor had shared his plans for the evening. With each word, Soriya's jaw had crept open more and more. She couldn't believe what he was suggesting, or that her aging teacher had a wide grin on his face the entire time.

Soriya had built up her final test in her mind. For her, it was the be-all, end-all of her training—a training that had started at the age of five and carried through every day, every conversation, and every interaction for the last thirteen years. She imagined a world-shattering threat to face, or an ancient puzzle to solve, something that demanded all her skills and wisdom to crack.

When Mentor didn't respond, her hand fell on his chest. "*Are* you kidding?"

Mentor sighed. "The rules are simple."

Soriya took a step back. "Hide-and-seek? Seriously?"

Her words boomed in the silence of the night. They were the only ones out and about at such a late hour, not that there were many along the strip known as the Corridor to begin with. The area had been an affordable housing project that never made it off the ground. The housing had been built too cheaply, yet had also cost too much at the same time. The result was a series of abandoned homes that did little but serve as squatter's dens and drug havens for those with nowhere else to turn. The businesses dotting the other side of the street had also been shuttered thanks to the bad press of the area. All the while, the Corridor kept the Courtyard hidden in plain view.

"The whole of the city is fair game," Mentor continued. He moved down the street, though his gait was staggered due to an injury to his right leg.

Soriya fell behind, still trying to wrap her thoughts around her final challenge. Thirteen years of study, yet the last test Mentor chose was a children's game?

"You may hide however you choose," Mentor said. He stopped at a lone bench on the side of the road and sat in the middle. His hands rested on his legs. "You can stay stationary, though I know it's not your style, or you can keep moving. If I find you, if I see you for even an instant, you lose."

Soriya scoffed. "Like that will happen."

Mentor's finger rose in warning. "You don't have to accept this challenge, Soriya. This is your final test to prove you're ready to fully take on the mantle of the Greystone. If you feel you're not ready or are frightened by my significant seeking abilities—"

"Wait," Soriya interrupted. "Significant seeking abilities?"

Mentor grinned. "I *always* find you, little one. Remember our games at home?"

"There was nowhere to hide!" Soriya exclaimed.

Their home consisted of an underground junction off the subway. The Bypass chamber was little more than a wide open space with a small domicile tucked in the corner. There were four rooms with no doors and no privacy. She had fought for a curtain in their makeshift bathroom, but little else was provided when it came to solitude... or hiding.

The memory caused her to grin nonetheless. Mentor had never been known for his sentimentality, but she recalled on many occasions catching him smile at their fun.

Mentor waved away her accusation, clearly unwilling to concede her point. "Whatever excuses you need to feel better about losing to your betters."

"Oh, it is on," Soriya replied.

Mentor stood and held out his hand. "So you agree to the challenge?"

"Hell yeah," Soriya said. She took the outstretched hand and gave it a hard shake. She stopped at the sight of his grimace.

"Soriya."

She rolled her eyes. He might have pretended to be anything but a parent, yet his lessons always held the same sting and carried the same weight. "I mean... yes, sir."

Mentor nodded and rounded the bench. He reached beneath and retrieved a single brown paper bag. Soriya watched, wondering what other surprises were in store for her. Carefully, he removed a lone object and placed it on the bench before her.

"What's that for?" She pointed to what appeared to be an oversized novelty hourglass. Sand sat on the lower end, stray granules filtering from the top. It stood three-feet tall and was wider than Mentor's fist.

He flipped the hourglass over. "This is your head start. It should give you about an hour."

Soriya peered closer as the thin stream of sand began to tick away the seconds. "Where do you buy a giant hourglass in Portents?"

"An interesting question," Mentor said. "Would you like to hear the answer?"

"I almost would."

"But?" He tracked her stare at the plummeting sand. "The clock is ticking, little one."

Soriya grinned. She reached out and punched Mentor's upper arm playfully. "See you in the morning, old man."

"Not if I see you first."

Soriya's laughter filled the Corridor and echoed down the block. She broke into a run, racing ahead into the growing darkness of the city. This was it: the final test. One night to prove to herself and to Mentor that she was ready to be the Greystone. That she was ready to protect her city with everything she had, every ounce of will and spirit. It came down to a game of hide-and-seek. There was no way in hell she was losing.

The game was on.

CHAPTER FIVE

Soriya's laughter stayed with him long after her departure from the Corridor. Mentor remained at the bench, eyeing the falling sand from the novelty hourglass he had found on a recent excursion downtown. He thought it set the mood perfectly for their night ahead.

Mentor beamed with pride at the thought of his ward. She had stuck by his side through every horror Portents had thrown at them over the years. Soriya had never asked for anything in that time, not friends, not vacations, not a single luxury afforded the youth of the world. Her only goal had been to study and learn everything he'd laid before her. She wanted to know about the myths and legends—the secrets of Portents—and the truth behind faith and religion. So much had been put on her shoulders, and she had taken it all in stride.

That had been especially true of late. It had been over a year since the Minotaur had visited the city. He had nearly ripped them apart in his effort to conquer what he'd believed to be a new labyrinth. Mentor still felt the effects of the creature's brutal assault along his right knee; the injury had never quite healed completely. Shiva and the Raktabija had brought with them their own pain and misery to Portents. How Soriya had found the strength to stand up to such enemies, such darkness, astounded Mentor. She was so young, yet so full of life and hope.

She had battled each threat in turn, without hesitation. Sure, Soriya had had help; she'd used tactics Mentor had questioned and railed against at the time. But her way had worked. She'd kept the city safe from danger and had come out the other side.

17

Mentor continued to worry about her. Part of his concern came from Kali. The deity had seen his death through the Bypass, a vision he had witnessed himself. With it came Soriya's own demise. It was a circumstance Mentor had never thought possible, a scenario so heartbreaking that he almost crumbled in defeat. There would be dark times ahead, challenges beyond any they had faced before. He knew better than to try to keep Soriya from them and shelter her from the world.

It didn't mean he couldn't try. That was where the hide-and-seek game originated. The night's so-called challenge was meant to bring back some of his student's joy; it was a chance for Soriya to have a night of fun in the city they worked so hard to protect.

Mentor stood, a smile on his lips. He too, hoped for a modicum of fun from the exercise. There would always be a new threat to face, but this night it would just be the two of them. That was how it had been at the beginning, when he saved a young girl from life as an orphan. He had sought only to protect her from a life of derision from children and adults alike. The other residents of Saint Helena's Orphanage had sensed how different Soriya was. They could not comprehend her unique view of the world. Mentor had recognized it immediately, however, and it warmed his heart.

It still did, even after all those years of training. There had been plenty of fights, especially during the teenage years— though it could have been much worse. No, he had been lucky to have Soriya at his side, and he hoped to show her that with one last test.

Mentor rounded the bench patiently as the thin grains of sand poured to the bottom of the hourglass. It signaled the end of his time as the city's protector; it was something he'd never believed possible when he started decades earlier. Soriya would be the Greystone, the first line of defense against the monsters in the city. He would merely be her teacher and her friend.

Somewhere along the way, Mentor had grown to accept the change to come. It was Soriya's time. She had earned the task a thousand times over through her words and her deeds.

Tonight was for her. It was for them. Mentor waited for the sand to fall, so he could join in the fun of their game.

CHAPTER SIX

The stop wasn't necessary. If the marketplace on Allure hadn't been so close to the Corridor, it probably wouldn't have popped up on Soriya's radar in the first place. It had been ten minutes since she left Mentor, yet Soriya still had no plan of attack. She had no real strategy when it came to hiding in Portents for the night.

Her only goal was to win.

Nothing else mattered—at least until she noticed Eddie Domingo through the window of the antique repair shop. Surrounding her was the rest of the Allure marketplace, a district lost to time. Many forgotten legends had settled into the area. They had attempted to live out their days in relative peace, while providing a service to the residents of the city. They were the cobblers, the butchers, and the grocers of Portents.

And then there was Eddie.

He had never struck her as the handyman type. After their last encounter, she'd believed he would depart the city as quickly as possible. That was more his style: running away from the fight rather than standing up for himself.

Eddie had proven her wrong. He stayed.

Soriya found him to be nothing but a miserable layabout when they'd met. He was not a selfless soul. Eddie Domingo had been the opposite, in fact. He had lived only for himself and was a crook and a liar. Theft had been his specialty, though what that equated to in life never amounted to much. Eddie had been pretty terrible at everything he'd ever attempted.

When she'd first learned of his possession of the shop, Soriya had had to see it for herself. She'd stuck to the shadows across the street, watching from a distance as he toiled within the confines of the corner business. He had cursed the restoration of an antique clock. Tools had flown through the air in frustration. Yet, Eddie had stayed. He'd pushed through his anger, his uselessness, and finished the work. She had watched him for hours, until it was completed and the clock sat on the shelf—a beacon of his hard work.

Soriya made a point to visit when time allowed. It was never for a face-to-face conversation, though. Something always kept her from wanting to upset the young man set on a new path.

Tonight, however, felt different. Soriya stepped up the small stoop out front and reached for the door. A small bell chimed when the door opened, and Soriya made her way inside.

The smell of wood shavings and glue filled her senses. Rare and beautiful antiques sat on shelves which lined the walls. It had been that way since the shop opened, thanks to the original proprietor. His name was Hephaestus, the master forger of legend, though he'd kept the distinction to himself. Using his special—and incredibly powerful—hammer for inspiration, the god had been able to create wonders and forge miracles for the good of his clientele.

Eddie had inherited the hammer with the god's passing. He had taken it upon himself to continue Hephaestus' good work. Guilt had been involved in the decision, of that Soriya had no doubt. Eddie had been responsible for the man's death.

Guilt might have been the start of it, but Soriya saw something more in his motivation. There was a change for the better she hoped he recognized and appreciated. Very few were afforded such chances in life.

Rolling shelves took up the center of the shop. Each contained the recent work of the craftsman. Dolls, puppets, clocks, and more helped shield her from view as Soriya moved deeper into the shop. Trinkets and treasures appeared to take up much of the man's time. It had clearly been a long week for him from the way his body slumped over the back counter.

"Can I help you?" Eddie called from behind the counter. He kept his back to her while he worked on the delicate watch in front of him. She caught his reflection in the mirror over the rear hallway of the shop as he carefully inserted a small cog within the gold-trimmed antique.

Soriya didn't bother to answer. She continued toward the counter, unable to take her eyes off the man. He was larger and more muscular than he had been before, though his frame was still lean. His hair was neatly trimmed, and his cheeks were flecked with stubble.

Her lack of response caused him to lower his tools to the bench. His left hand crept beneath the counter for a lone object leaning along the corner. She could see it clearly from the mirror.

A hammer.

Eddie had forged the weapon with the help of Hephaestus' mythic tool. Just when his fingers cradled the end of the broad handle, she cleared her throat to stop him. "Don't even think about it, Eddie."

Eddie nearly jumped at the sound of her voice. His hand fell away from the hammer, and his shoulders slumped further. He turned to greet her, and she spotted irritation in his tired eyes.

"Well, well," he intoned. "If it isn't my very own parole officer. What brings you to my neck of the woods? Tired of scaring children out of their lunch money?"

She had forgotten his wit and incredible lack of charm. His reaction to her arrival brought a sly grin to her face. "It's good to see you, too." Soriya cocked her head toward the hammer in the corner. "Not so much that. Shouldn't you keep that in the forge or locked away?"

Eddie lifted the hammer and plopped it on the counter between them. His fingers grazed the hilt. "Nay. It helps take care of the roaches when necessary."

"Now there's a useful application for a tool that took out the Minotaur."

Eddie sighed. "It's not like I'm using it to break into banks, Soriya. I keep my nose clean, I work in my shop, and I mind my own business."

"I know, Eddie."

"That why you're here?" he asked, the question sharp. "Why

you've been watching me?"

He knew. Even when she'd kept her distance, somehow he had noticed her presence. She had tried to be discrete, to give him the space he'd earned through his help with the fabled creature. Disappointment filled his face; he was clearly hurt at the thought she had been keeping an eye on him.

"Is that what you think?" She hadn't expected the look of betrayal in his eyes. Soriya stepped closer and reached out toward him. "Eddie, I try to watch everyone."

Eddie pulled away. He settled against the back workbench, hands clutched tight to the edge. "I didn't ask for a babysitter."

Soriya nodded. "Wasn't my intention."

"You sure about that?"

Soriya held back a reply. She hadn't come to argue. She tapped the glass of the counter, then took a step for the exit. "You're doing good things here, Eddie. That's all I came to say."

He couldn't even look at her, his eyes locked on the hammer and the floor. "Got it. Thanks."

Soriya waited for more. Nothing else was forthcoming from the man. She had hoped for a better reunion, a fresh start for the pair. Instead, she had made things worse.

"I'll leave you to it."

The bell chimed and the breeze swirled around her as Soriya exited the shop. Eddie settled against the counter and turned back to his work, leaving his visitor and their exchange behind.

She really was proud of him, of his ability to change after a life filled with family obligation and lawlessness. She had meant to show that to him with her visit, but he wanted none of it. It was almost like he didn't see the change at all.

Soriya hesitated outside, pondering a return to the shop to fix things. The clock at the corner, however, drew her attention. The past would have to wait. Her future was all that mattered at the moment. And her hour head start was running out.

CHAPTER SEVEN

Soriya left the marketplace at Allure and shifted downtown through the bright lights of Evans Avenue. She cut southeast, heading for the port. Along the way, she found herself pausing in the quiet of a small business district just south of the coves.

It made her grin. No, not the emptiness of the storefront or the graffiti-laden brick walls. She smiled at the fact she had landed in yet another part of town she hadn't expected to visit—especially tonight of all nights.

She hadn't been to the alley since the fight with the Minotaur. She and Mentor had carried the beast to his home in the labyrinth hidden just behind the back wall between businesses. Every trace of the ancient maze had been covered up afterward.

Soriya traveled to the deepest recesses of the alley. Her hand ran along the brick that hid the marble columns and the torchlight from view. She pressed her ear to the wall. Her eyes closed while she listened for the sound of the mighty beast's hooves stomping through the maze. Had he looked for her since his incarceration? Had he tried to escape to face her once more?

The Minotaur had been her first true test. He had challenged her and threatened the lives of everyone around her, wanting the chance to run free through the streets of Portents. There had been a time she'd thought him impossible to defeat, that all of her training had been for nothing. She'd believed that the role of Greystone had been meant for someone stronger, wiser, and more prepared.

She had done it, though. She had survived. More than that, Soriya had blossomed thanks to that encounter—as well as the threat of the Raktabija and Shiva soon after. She had fought against impossible odds, beaten them all, and won.

Soriya opened her eyes. The thought of her victory soothed her. It cleansed her of the remaining doubts in her system. People changed, even if someone like Eddie failed to see it. She certainly had over the years. The burden of the role had merely been another challenge to overcome. It was a weight she looked forward to carrying day in and day out, for as long as she was able to.

The darkness receded behind her. A light flared in the distance, and a dim green hue rose from the street. "That light," Soriya muttered. She turned from the past and started toward the glow. "I've seen that light before."

While she passed an empty storefront adjacent to the alley, Soriya recalled the sign that had been there during her last visit. It had belonged to a local campaign of some kind, yet had since been shuttered and vacant.

The light, however, came from across the way. It beamed above and below the thin veil of a curtain that hid the contents of the shop. A broom lay across the window, and the name WICCAN NEEDS was in bold letters atop.

Soriya had seen the same glow before. The light had signaled the return of not one but two grave threats to Portents. The green hue also reminded her of the Bypass. Somehow, someone had found a way to pierce the veil to other worlds without direct access to the Bypass. Whoever it was had unwittingly freed the Minotaur from captivity and had also set Shiva loose from the Svarga Loka.

"Another door."

Soriya raced over to the store and peered through the small gap at the edge of the curtain. A woman sat before a ring of salt. Her legs were crossed, and her features were heavily shadowed thanks to the green cloak she wore. Her chants echoed in the space. Small candles flickered in green as an orb of light grew in the center of the summoning circle.

"She's making another door."

Soriya couldn't take the chance. She couldn't sit back and wait for something else to step through the door and lay waste to her city.

"Not tonight," Soriya said, taking two large steps back to the edge of the sidewalk. Her fists balled up at her sides. "Not ever again."

She ran for the store. Leaping, Soriya plunged her fists forward and crashed through the window. Her hand swiped at the curtain, knocking it away as she landed in front of the cloaked woman.

The girl fell back, the chant on her lips silenced by Soriya's arrival. Her eyes widened in terror. "What the hell?"

The green orb between them spun wildly. Small flickers of light spun off in all directions. Soriya ignored them, shifting closer toward the woman. "Not another word, lady, or—"

Her foot slipped slightly. The salt barrier under her heel separated for an instant with her step. The green glow hovered in front of Soriya for a brief moment. The orb spun violently, the light shifting brighter with each rotation. Then, it shot out through the broken window and into the night air.

Soriya spun to watch the dim afterglow. The orb was gone as quickly as it had arrived.

"Oh. Oh, no." The voice came from behind her. The cloaked woman was on her knees. Soriya noted the terror in her eyes. The woman pointed to the intruder in her shop. Her other hand covered her trembling lips. "What... what have you just done?"

CHAPTER EIGHT

Evans Tower stood at the heart of Portents. The eighty-six-floor obsidian spire served as a reminder of the city's origin and the future it carved along the passage of time. At the back of the building were four oversized loading bays. During the day, dozens worked the area, lifting massive pallets of products to be sent out. Every product carried the Evans name. Evans had its hand in every facet of life, from household items to computer servers to office furniture.

At night, however, the bay doors were locked, and all activity faded to silence. The rare security guard surveyed the perimeter to keep an eye out, though few ever strayed near the black beacon of shadow.

Lenny Perkins held the distinct honor of night watchman. He was a short, unattractive shlub of a man who hated the job. Sure, there were perks when it came to sitting in the office and staring at monitors, and there was plenty of time to catch up on his shows; he was currently subscribed to more than three hundred YouTube channels. Why he cared about skateboarding spills or the newest burger creation at a chain nowhere near Portents, he didn't know, but he kept watching for no other reason than he didn't have anything else to do with his time.

But outside the security room, there was nothing Lenny enjoyed about the work, because nothing ever happened. His nightly patrol always caused his uniform to ride up in all the wrong areas. Then there was the constant shift in the weather. Lenny never knew if he was walking into a tundra or if he'd come back covered in sweat. It was a needless worry when he would rather find out the latest true crime mystery as told by a C-list celebrity with no acting chops, or listen to a podcast interview about what new shows were premiering in the fall. He had priorities, yet work always managed to get in the way. There was excitement in his viewing, whereas his life—the job of the great night watchman at Evans Tower—bored the shit out of him.

It was the end of another circuit of the building when the light appeared. The green orb shot through the air and spun uncontrollably between buildings. It stopped at times, circling overhead, before darting east then west down entire blocks. Awareness seemed to hit the mysterious object, and the orb curved back toward the tower. It crashed toward the ground like a meteor, then halted six feet above. The spinning slowed, and the light grew.

Lenny stood in awe of the green glow. His radio chirped for an update, but he ignored the sound of his colleagues. Everything in the world faded except for the orb.

The light spread, and with it, the sphere. It touched the earth and solidified, forming a large arch in the center of the loading bay area. Within the bright luminescence, forms started to take shape. Three figures reached out of the light and entered the world. Their screams filled the air. When each slipped from the light, they cried out in pain as if expelled from the other side.

Lenny, suddenly fearful for his life, dipped into the shadows at the corner of the tower. He hugged tight to the building. Sweat slid down his cheeks and settled into his eyes. He couldn't look away at the three figures in front of him.

They were women, or they had been at one point. Each had the grace and curvature of the female form, beneath deep green cloaks with golden glyphs decorating the sleeves. None of them had arrived with any trace of beauty though. Instead, they were hideously deformed. One had no eyes. Skin had grown over the sockets instead—stretched and translucent in texture. Small punctures dotted her palms, holes upon her skin that appeared to breathe in and out at the same frequency as her rising chest.

The second was even more terrifying. Wild eyes flitted from object to object, never able to focus on any one item. Her mouth had been sewn shut and stapled for good measure. It didn't stop the sound of growling emanating from her being, almost like a mental scream pushing against those around her. Her fingernails were overgrown and curved like claws. Her body was hunched, constantly shifting and unable to relax. She was more animal than human.

The final figure did not step from the light. She floated above the ground, hands outstretched with quiet dignity. She was old—ancient, even. Her emaciated skin stuck to her bones. Tiny beads of black stared ahead at the loading bays and the city beyond with contempt. With their arrival, the light faded from view.

"We are free," the floating woman declared.

The one without eyes waved her hand before her, almost sniffing the air. "The world, Mercy. I can sense the world again."

Too loud.' The words of the third weren't 'said,' due to her stapled lips, though somehow each one filled the air and beat against Lenny's mind as if shouted. *'Crashing. Banging.'*

A raised finger from Mercy halted the rambling woman. The relentless shifting stopped. "Quiet yourself, Maggie dear. There will be time for your mania later."

Mercy landed on the ground and started for the former position of the glowing, green orb. The others followed her closely.

"What is it, Mercy?" the eyeless one asked.

"What's happened to us?" Mercy replied. She held out her hands, clearly disgusted by the look of them. "Free we might be, but the cost? Centuries of beauty ripped from us. *Centuries* taken from us."

'Changed!' screamed the mind of Maggie. *'Merely changed.'*

"The light called to us for a reason."

"You are right, Mary," Mercy admitted with a bowed head. "You as well, Maggie, in your own way."

"How?" Mary asked. "This place? It is different, yet I can still feel it as if not a second has passed. This place—"

"Is where we died so long ago," Mercy confirmed.

'Betrayed!' Maggie shouted, her eyes wide with anger.

"The light returned us," Mercy said. She reached out, like she was trying to catch the remnants of the orb long since departed.

"I have seen that light before."

"I sense it," Mary said as her hands danced in the air.

'Power.' Maggie called through her disparate thoughts. *'Wild. Growing.'*

"Power to send us back," Mercy said. Her hand snatched at the emptiness before her. Fingers locked tight against her palm, squeezing the air in her grasp. "Or, power to use—to bend to our needs."

Mary nodded. "I can feel it, Sister."

Mercy's black eyes pierced the night. "Then by all means, Sister… lead us."

All three left the ground, floating like angelic terrors on the night wind. They headed east where the light had come from. Lenny Perkins could only stand watch, ever the observer and never the man of action he dreamed he was while watching his favorite shows.

It would be a long time before he looked at the world the same way again. A longer time still before he would complain of being bored with his mundane existence.

CHAPTER NINE

This can't be happening.

Annabelle fought to find her voice. The insane woman, who had just jumped through her shop's window and disrupted months of hard work, was still yelling at her. Glass scattered through the room. Potions and holistic remedies were tipped over on their shelves, some dangling precariously along the edges thanks to the wind blowing in from outside. Her privacy curtain hung by a thread along the rod and snapped in the breeze.

She had planned everything out so perfectly—from the time of the ceremony, to the supplies required. She had practiced the incantations for weeks. Books surrounded her for reference to prevent any mistakes. There shouldn't have been any issues.

Then *she* showed up.

The woman completely disregarded the wardings on the door and the walls. The intruder also missed the massive glyphs painted on the floor. The writing was surrounded by the salt circle to ensnare any and all magical incursions during the ceremony.

The circle had been broken, however, when the woman's sneaker had slid through the barrier. In that moment, the salt line had been shattered, and with it all sense of containment. The spell's energy spilled out the second she'd entered.

Annabelle knocked back the hood to her cloak and jumped to her feet. "Look at what you've done!"

The woman fell to her heels. Her hand settled along her chest and her eyes widened in surprise. "What *I've* done? Do you have any idea what you're playing with here? The forces you were calling—"

"Were under control," Annabelle snapped. "And I wasn't *playing* at anything. If anyone is to blame, it's you."

"Me? I probably saved you."

Annabelle shook her head. She pointed to the broken salt line. "You disrupted the spell."

"Good," the woman replied with satisfaction.

"*Not* good," Annabelle shot back. She groaned in frustration. "Not good at all. Terrible—dangerous, even. All that energy had to go somewhere, and thanks to you it wasn't *here* where I was prepared to contain the situation."

The anger in the intruder's eyes melted for a moment as concern set in. "What are you saying?"

"A door opened," Annabelle answered. She pointed outside. "Somewhere out there."

The woman snatched the collar of Annabelle's cloak and pulled her close. Spit flew from her lips. "A door to where? Tell me!"

It had happened the first time as well. Annabelle had thought she'd planned for every contingency, but the spell was too powerful. Her wardings had failed to contain the door, and it spilled out into the city. That time it had not gone far, merely to the alley across the street. But when the Minotaur stepped forth, Annabelle had realized the price of her error. This time, though, she had no clue what was coming.

"I don't know!" she yelled. She ripped free from the woman's grasp. "You interrupted the incantation. I spent months getting it *just* right. This… this was my chance."

"At what?"

The woman reached for her again, but Annabelle swatted the woman's hand away. "Back off."

"No," her attacker spat. She trailed Annabelle's movements deeper into the shop. The woman matched every step Annabelle took. "Not until you tell me everything. About you. About the door. Now."

"I don't owe you anything. I'm not even sure if it worked."

"Oh, it did, my dear," a voice called from outside.

Both turned as three hideously deformed women soared effortlessly into the shop. They floated above the ground, over the summoning glyph, graceful and terrifying in the same instant.

"My God," Annabelle muttered.

Her attacker split the room in two, arms wide to cut the newcomers off from Annabelle. "Stay behind me."

"What is this?" Annabelle asked.

Her entire night had been built up for one thing, yet it had become something else entirely. Every hope, every desire, had been focused on finding her home and her family so she could better understand who she was meant to be.

"Who are they?" Annabelle's question fell on deaf ears. The woman, now attempting to protect her rather than throttle her, clearly had no answers. Neither of them had any clue about the newcomers hovering above them or the power that seemed to permeate the shop with their arrival.

The pair continued to back away from the open space at the front of the shop. They stopped between shelves of glass containers filled with extracts and herbs Annabelle had collected from all over the city. Annabelle grabbed the woman's shoulder. She needed a calm word or some sign of understanding. The dark-skinned warrior only shook her head.

"I'll handle this."

"I don't even know what *this* is," Annabelle whispered.

The woman in the lead, with the emaciated form of a skeleton and a pair of beady black eyes that sucked the light from the room, landed on the ground. Her bony fingers extended for the pair, though her gaze looked right through to Annabelle.

"We simply wanted to thank you for your help, Sister."

'Alive again,' a voice called out. The woman with the sewn lips was speaking directly to Annabelle's mind. The intensity of the experience caused her to clamp down on her ears. *'Free again.'*

The emaciated woman in the green cloak approached slowly, hands open and welcoming. "Please allow us to return the favor."

CHAPTER TEN

Soriya couldn't believe her luck. Ever since the Minotaur had made his way into her city, she'd been on the lookout for the person able to open doors between worlds. With the arrival of Shiva, she'd realized that it wasn't just a matter of opening the door. Somehow this individual had managed to tap into the fundamental nature of the Bypass itself. They had found a way to connect to all of time and space, past and present, to create the breaches. A simple search wasn't enough to end the potential threat of someone with such a power—it had become a manhunt.

Months had been lost scouring the city for some shred of evidence about the person responsible for bringing such nightmares to Portents. Soriya had turned to every resource available for insight as to where someone might go to hone such a talent.

Now Soriya had found her. This witch had unwittingly allowed a new threat to emerge from one of her errant doors. For all her talents with tapping into the Bypass to open her doors, the woman seemed incapable of loosing anything but the horrors of existence.

"They... they're monsters," the scarlet-locked woman whispered.

The woman wasn't wrong. All three were gruesome in appearance. Their return had no doubt been painful. Mentor had mentioned cases like theirs. They were escapees from the depths of the Bypass. The process tended to be costly, from the rending of flesh to the splitting of souls. It was meant to serve as a deterrent, but the truly desperate somehow always managed to find a way to come back.

Despite their deformities, Soriya sensed the power emanating from them. It appeared to flow from their bodies like an aura, growing with each passing moment as they reacclimated to their surroundings.

"You shouldn't say that about potential customers," Soriya said. She continued to inch backward through the shop. She kept the terrified woman behind her, acting as a human shield. Soriya cocked her head to the woman cowering at her back. "But yeah, they are definitely not looking their best."

"These forms came at a cost," the black-eyed spokeswoman for the group said. "A price to pay for our former arrogance."

'Betrayed,' the one with no mouth wordlessly uttered. Her mental voice was like nails being driven directly into Soriya's brain. Everyone in the room felt the same, shifting to cover their ears. *'Ruined.'*

The one without eyes pointed to the woman. The puncture wounds along her palm opened and closed as if they filled the void for her sightlessness. "The girl holds power." Her hand shifted toward Soriya. "They both do."

Soriya smirked. "Damn right I do."

She opened the pouch at her side. The small stone within slid against her palm, warm to the touch. Soriya held the weapon before her for all to see.

'Greystone!' the shifting mind of the mouthless woman shouted.

"We did not come for violence, protector," the emaciated woman said. "We merely came to offer our thanks."

"You've said it, then," Soriya replied. "Don't let the door hit you on the way out."

"I'm afraid we won't be leaving without the girl."

Soriya sighed. "Kind of had a feeling you would say that."

"Sister…" the hollow-eyed creature said.

Their leader sneered, raising her hands before her. "Consider it done, Sister."

"Consider what—"

Soriya never finished the question. The emaciated woman flicked her finger to the left. The simple act caused all Soriya's control over her own body to fail her in an instant. Her arms fell to her sides and tucked tight against her body. Soriya turned, unable to stop herself, then shot through the air. She crashed through shelving. Glass samples of potions and herbs broke and shattered. Soriya's body continued to sail until it reached the back wall of the shop. She bounced off the plaster and slammed face-first into the ground.

"We didn't come to fight," the witch said. She landed before the scarlet-haired woman. "We simply wanted to have a chat, my dear."

"No, thank you."

"Oh, we insist," the bony figure replied.

The other two landed on either side of the woman and grabbed at her arms. The doormaker swatted at their touch. "Get away from me!"

Soriya shook off the effects of her unexpected trip across the store. The power in such a simple move was staggering to her. Despite all the beasts Soriya had faced, she had never been overwhelmed so effortlessly. The realization set in: they could have easily ended her life. The fact that Soriya was still breathing had been an error in judgment on their part. It was one she couldn't allow them to rectify.

Since she was too far away to rescue the woman she had come to stop, Soriya let the ribbon wrapped along her left arm slip loose. It unfurled to the floor, one end still tied to her wrist.

Soriya stood to face the trio. "The lady is spoken for to-night."

The ribbon of Kali snapped through the air. Sensing the strike, the eyeless attacker dove out of the way. The ribbon didn't hesitate and seemed to have a mind of its own. Pink strands snatched the redhead's arm. Secured on both ends, Soriya pulled and the doormaker sailed toward her. Soriya caught the woman as the ribbon retracted back into place along her arm.

"Sorry you didn't get the message," Soriya said with a widening grin.

"How did you—"

"Questions later," Soriya snapped at the woman. She set her

down, then pushed her for the exit. "Now run."

"Get them!" the emaciated sister bellowed.

Soriya and the woman skirted through the back storeroom, darting between rows of goods meticulously labeled and organized. The trio soared after them, bloodlust in their eyes—at least the two that had eyes. When Soriya made it outside, she halted and spun around on her heels.

The Greystone was in her hand and ready. She channeled her will into the ancient weapon. "Not this time."

"What are you doing?" the woman at her back asked.

Soriya remained silent while she focused all her strength into the stone. Beneath them, the street shuddered. Rumbling spread from their position for the store. Cracks formed in the road, deep and widening as they raced for the main supports of the structure.

"Hey!" the woman shouted. "Stop! What are you—"

The tremors grew. Walls shook from Soriya's effort, then began the crumble in on themselves. The entire back room of the store collapsed, burying their pursuers in rubble.

"My shop!"

Soriya staggered forward a step—the effort had been tremendous. Stability returned to the street. The stone was cool against her skin.

The fear remained on the redhead's face. Now it was accentuated with pure horror at the scene before her. The shop had been hers, and the work had obviously been important to her. Soriya hadn't considered that. She had only sought a way for them to survive.

"How's your insurance?" Soriya asked, hoping to lighten the woman's spirits. "I probably should have asked before I did that."

The woman crept closer. The sound of crumbling supports

continued to settle in the heap that had been the back room of her shop. She stood in shock at the destruction. Neither one had the time for it.

Soriya pulled at her companion. "We need to keep moving. That will only slow them down."

The woman hesitated, then offered a slight nod. The pair took off down the street in a run. Two blocks out, the witch found her voice again. She stopped short at the intersection of Waters and Devlin.

"Where?" she said. "Where are we going?" Soriya tried to force the woman to keep moving. Instead, she stopped completely. "That's enough! I need answers."

"So do I." Soriya skidded to a halt. Her chest heaved. Their diversion would not last much longer. They needed a place to hide, somewhere to regroup and figure out more about the threat unleashed on Portents.

The lights of downtown provided a clear path ahead and an answer. Soriya snapped her fingers, then waved for the woman to follow as she picked up the pace once more.

"Come on," Soriya said. "I think I know a good place to start."

CHAPTER ELEVEN

Debris shifted and shuffled from the collapsed shop. Loose brick and crumbling masonry crashed to the street. Beneath the destruction, support beams strained to keep the massive weight of the collapse off the three inhabitants.

Mercy raised her bony, tendril-like fingers to the roof. Light beamed from the tips. With a single thought, the debris shot out and spread away from their hideaway inside. Brick and tile gave way to open sky as peace returned to the sleepy block.

With fresh air flooding into the confined space, Mercy turned to the back exit barred by shattered shelving and snapped her fingers. The remains of the room crumbled; each piece of wood and every piece of accumulated debris turned to dust to reveal the exit. The sisters departed, stopping just outside. They scanned the street hurriedly.

'Escaped,' Maggie shouted. *The power. Gone.'*

Mary waved her hands through the air in an attempt to sense their presence. Anger seeped into her graceful movements. Her fingers clenched tight to her palms as she turned to the raving sister.

"This is all your fault, Maggie!" she snapped. "If it wasn't for your ineptitude, they wouldn't—"

'Me?' Maggie said. *'You! No eyes. Cannot see. Never could!'*

"You—" Bolts of light flew freely between them. Each sister screamed from the effort. Maggie ducked below the strike, and Mary batted her sister's efforts aside as if they were nothing but air. Their stray shots lit small fires along the pavement and within the scattered remains of the shop.

Mercy watched the debacle with contempt. Her patience had ended the moment the roof collapsed on them and the second they'd lost sight of their goal. Her sisters had always had that effect on her. She had hoped a second chance at life would change their dynamic; instead, it seemed to accentuate their faults more and more.

The head of their makeshift trio sighed. She shifted between them, attracting each of their attacks in turn. Light slapped at her, but none of it affected her. She merely absorbed them. The energy coated her skin like a shield.

"That is enough!" Mercy yelled.

Her sisters huffed in aggravation.

Mary turned away from the spat. Her hand extended down the road to scan the area. "What can we do now? Track her? Follow their movements through this strange place?"

"It's not strange," Mercy explained. It might have seemed that way, but they knew the truth. This was Portents. It might have grown and expanded over the centuries, but at its heart, the city remained the same as it ever was.

'Home.' Maggie mirrored Mercy's thoughts.

"That's right, Sister," Mercy agreed. She turned to the frustrated Mary. "We could track them. However, there are other ways to achieve our goals. You recognized her companion?"

Maggie nodded. 'Stone bearer. Supposed to protect. This one fights us. Hurts us.'

"It *was* the stone," Mary said. "The one from old. The one from the beginning."

Mercy saw that much clearly. The moment the warrior had stood against them and held tight to her weapon, Mercy knew who their opponent was. Mercy also knew how to deal with her.

"A Greystone," she said. "Ever the protector."

'Send us back, she will!' Maggie mentally shouted. Her movements were manic. 'Burn us! Hurt us!'

Mercy raised a hand in an effort to calm Maggie. "If we strike directly, yes. But indirectly?"

Mercy's glare bore down on her young sibling. Understanding took hold, and Maggie grinned, the staples on her lips stretching. They dug deeper into her skin and caused blood to seep from the edges in tiny drops.

'Chaos,' she said, excitement behind the word. *'Panic.'*

"A distraction," Mary said.

Mercy beckoned the others to follow her back into the shop. They stepped through the destruction at the rear of the store until they returned to the display counters and unaffected shelves at the front. Her hands spread wide between the countless items collected by the proprietor.

"It appears we have everything we need," she said to her sisters. "How convenient for us."

"And disastrous for them," Mary answered with a laugh.

Maggie lifted a bottle of mandrake root. *'Fun. Amusement.'*

Mercy took the bottle and held it before Maggie. "A means to an end, dear. Remember that."

She returned the bottle, then started in on the other shelves. They picked at the contents through the shop, collecting ingredients as they went. There was no need for instructions. They were sisters, after all, and their goal was clear.

The doormaker was the key. She was guarded, however. It was time to give her protector something new to worry about. They required a distraction, one worthy of their unique talents. It would serve as a welcome home to the city they helped found.

They set to work bringing their plans to light.

CHAPTER TWELVE

Urg saw the bad night coming the second he realized he'd picked up the wrong dry cleaning order. After that mishap had been cleared up and his clothes retrieved, there was the missed bus that forced him to run twelve blocks so he wouldn't be late for work. He changed clothes in the restroom of Night Owls, the bar he worked at as a bouncer, before the crowds showed up.

As he left the bathroom to take up his position at the door, Urg's jacket sleeve caught on the jamb and ripped. At the sound, his head fell to his chest. He didn't bother to look at the sleeve to see the extent of the damage.

He just wanted the day to be over.

The clock read 1:13. Almost three hours remained in his shift. Three hours of sitting in front of the door at Night Owls and carding people willing to risk the shadows in the city. Some of those people brought a smile to his face. Most, though, brought nothing but aggravation.

Urg did his best to not brood over his ruined jacket. He tried to at least, but when he thought of his dwindling wardrobe, he couldn't help but grimace. The kid in front of him wasn't helping matters. He was clearly two years early to the party. He wore his hair down over his forehead and kept his eyes to the ground, likely to give Urg a hard time checking the ID.

"This is supposed to be you?" Urg asked, his deep voice immediately causing the kid to stand upright.

The kid continued to play with his hair. The reason was easy to figure out: the picture depicted the cropped cut of a man in his mid-twenties. The kid before him had it grown out to his shoulders. Color was the same. While the facial features were similar, they were not exact.

"Uh, yeah," the kid said, still unable to make eye contact with the bouncer.

Urg handed back the license. "Kid, I've never seen an ID so chalked up before."

"It's old," the kid shot back, his voice high and whiny.

Urg rose from his stool. He towered over the boy with the overgrown hair and the baby voice. "Older than you, probably. Take a walk."

The kid hung his head low, he jammed his hands in his pockets, and kicked at the pavement. "Man…"

Urg grumbled as he sat back down on his stool. He shook his head, and a sigh escaped his lips. The next person in line walked up to him. She wore knee-high boots and a jean skirt. Her purple top was low-cut, showing off ample cleavage, yet it left plenty to the imagination. She wore ruby red lipstick, and her raven hair was tied off down the back of her neck.

"Kids these days." She passed off her license.

Urg took it in hand, not bothering to glance at it. He had known Rachel Sawyer for years. "That kid was you not that long ago, Rach, if I remember correctly."

"How could you at your age?" she joked.

Urg huffed at the comment. He flicked the ID at her and she caught it, then slipped the license into her shoulder bag. "Get in there before I change my mind."

"Thanks, Urg," she said. She moved in close for a hug, but stopped at the sight of his sleeve. "What happened to the jacket?"

"Life," Urg grumbled. "Have fun in there."

She ran her hand over his arm before heading inside. "Always."

He laughed as she left. Rachel had always been a strong-willed woman. Brazen—both in manner and dress—the young woman owned every room she stepped into. There was a confidence behind her eyes: the way she locked in on you from the word hello and stayed with you verbal jab for verbal jab no matter what the subject.

Rachel reminded him of Soriya in a lot of ways. It was as if they had been cut from the same cloth, like they shared some spiritual connection in the way they held themselves or how they treated people. Urg felt grateful to have Rachel in his life, and to have Soriya as well, though he hadn't seen her much since their run-in with Kali.

Urg finished with the last of the waiting guests. Most were granted access, and only a few needed a swift kick in the ass to vamoose. When the quiet returned to the front of Night Owls, Urg settled along the edge of the stool. His watch seemed to crawl to the next minute. It was going to be a long night.

Something in the distance stirred him from his gloominess. Night Owls occupied a very specific section of town, what most referred to as the red-light district, though the ambiance of the strip never warranted such a name. Bars and clubs took up most of the real estate. The few restaurants in the area never stayed open late—not in Portents. The unwritten rule of the town basically gave the alcohol-loving community free rein once the sun settled.

Down the way, doors crashed open. People splayed out on the pavement. Urg's brow furrowed and he stood for a better look. A mist rose up from the ground. Through the mist came more people. They vacated clubs; the sound of glass shattering accompanied their arrival. Growls rose, and a man snatched the hair of a woman from inside one of the clubs—*Vincent's*, Urg thought—before dragging her out through the window and onto the street.

The sounds grew louder as the incidents shifted closer and closer to Night Owls. People snarled at each other, dropping on all fours like animals. They sprinted back and forth between establishments. Those that didn't succumb to their baser instincts screamed and ran in all directions in a panic down the wide thoroughfare.

"Oh my God!" a woman shouted. Her hands flailed over her head as she bolted toward Urg. She was accompanied by a man at her side, who fled to save himself over all others.

"Run!" he bellowed as he passed Urg. "They've changed!

They—!"

A growl escaped the woman. She fell on her hands and feet, her limbs snapping as she turned feral right before Urg's eyes. The woman pounced on the fleeing man. She clawed at his shirt from atop him. Her eyes were red flames of fury, and her nails dug into the man's flesh.

"What the hell is this?" Urg asked. He started to move for the pair, but stopped when he noticed three figures hovering in the air.

"Humanity's true face, my dear orc," one said. She held tight to a jar containing the same mist he had seen rising from the street. She dropped it before him, and the other two women tossed theirs into the establishments surrounding them—including Night Owls.

Urg's world turned red as the woman grinned at him. "Enjoy the chaos."

CHAPTER THIRTEEN

The house sat in the midst of the spires of downtown. The intricately decorated palatial estate took up an entire block. Pillars dominated the front, and marble angel statues rested along the rooftop ledge overlooking the street. It didn't match the businesses of the area. Investment firms and conglomerates occupied much of the opposing block, stretching for as far as the eye could see. The home was unique in that regard, a throwback to an older time.

The home had belonged to Alexander Vertrum, one of the original settlers of Portents. He had built the structure with his own hands in the earliest days of the city, not far from the hustle and bustle of Evans Tower.

Vertrum was an author who chronicled the early years of Portents. His work documented the arrival of the first settlers. He had penned the first biography of the city's founder, William Rath, along with the accounts of a dozen other prominent figures. Those came later in his career and were overshadowed by work that had been deemed too controversial to share with the public. Most of those early publications had been lost to time. What had survived the passage of centuries had been described as a hopeful look at a time there had been little to be optimistic about.

A fire had claimed the rest of the man's legacy at the turn of the twenty-first century. The house had been rebuilt by the city, which transformed it to a historical site to honor the man's memory.

The first-floor windows were blacked out, and the level had

no entry points. The only way into the home was up the wide stairs and through the double doors to the second floor. When asked about the lower level, curators explained that it still contained the wreckage from the blaze and had been closed off rather than rehabilitated.

It was a lie.

Soriya reached the second-floor landing. The double doors to the Vertrum home were locked. A security keypad embedded in the wall next to the entrance beeped for a code. Soriya had none to give. Mentor might have known it, but he'd never shared that information with her. Instead, the young woman peeled the panel off the wall. Strength coursed through her body thanks to the stone in her hand. Soriya dislodged the wires tucked behind the panel. The lock clicked, and the door to the right creaked open from the frame.

Her companion said nothing of the exchange. The redhead with the green cloak followed close, clearly lost in thought. It was not the reaction Soriya typically endured when it came to her adventures. There was always some back and forth, some need for information as to where, or how, or even why things were happening. Some brought more questions and their own knowledge into the conversation like Beth had, while others complained incessantly like Eddie.

Soriya paused at the threshold of the Vertrum home. She missed her friends.

Stepping into the home, Soriya was transported to a different time. Though the outside had been updated in the reconstruction, over the decades the inside had shifted back to its original layout. It was a piece of history perfectly preserved after the fact.

Chandeliers hung from the high ceilings. Glass clinked with the sudden shift in the air that trailed their arrival. Stairs led to the third floor, and photos of historical figures decorated the wall opposite the wooden railing.

Soriya ushered her companion inside, then closed the door. She ran her finger over the surface of the stone in her hand.

Light beamed ahead to guide their path. To the left was the formal dining room. Exhibits surrounded the table in the center, which was decorated with table settings for a family meal. Vertrum had been known for his gatherings. They had always been an excuse to read from his latest manuscript or regale his guests with the exploits of the early days.

The man's study was on the right. An inkwell sat beside a piece of parchment on the desk in the corner. The windows next to the cozy space offered the perfect amount of light, though candles decorated the mantel as a precaution.

Everything in the home was meant to evoke a sense of the past. Every piece of furniture crafted for display and every exhibit shared with the public during business hours was about transporting people to a different era and inspiring them with the struggles of those early days. It was about optimism in the face of countless obstacles.

The truth behind the home was in what it hid beneath the surface. Or, in point of fact, below the public face of the manor.

Soriya led the cloaked woman down the corridor beside the stairwell. Boards creaked under their weight. They passed images of the founders: Patrick Hennessey, Wilbur Caldwell, and William Rath—though Rath's image seemed to change with the times rather than remain preserved the way the other men had been.

All stood together in a single portrait at the base of the stairs. It had been a gathering of all the founders around the table in Vertrum's dining room. They stood together, tall and proud. The men took the foreground of the image. William Rath stood in the center, as he always appeared. Caldwell and Hennessey were positioned at his right, with Vertrum on the left. They were the historical figures celebrated each year during the Founders Day parade. Women occupied the background, faded like their role in history. There was Vertrum's wife, of course, to one side along with the other wives. A small group of women was gathered to the right of the main crowd. They wore green cloaks, though their faces were too faded to recognize. One, however, still held a piercing gaze—emerald green eyes that stared ominously back at Soriya.

Soriya closed her eyes and shook her head. She wasn't sure how much time they had, nor how long they could stay hidden. Paneling dominated the wall except for the lone image of the founders. Soriya reached for the frame.

"What are you doing?" her companion asked.

"You'll see."

She pulled the image up from the hanger and away from the wall. Beneath the frame was a small, innocuous glyph etched into the paneling: a torch with a flame rising from the top. It was the symbol of the Luminaries. The sign could be found throughout the city, in almost every structure. The Luminaries hid their secrets well to protect knowledge from all.

Soriya handed the frame to her companion. The confused young woman held it for a moment before placing the photo on the floor behind her. Soriya's hand grazed the glyph on the wall, feeling each bend in the etching. Then she pushed in the center, and the square sunk into the paneling. When it fell flush with the wall, Soriya twisted the sigil clockwise until a loud click echoed in the corridor.

The paneling of the wall shifted. Each piece folded in over the next until the entire wall was removed to the farthest edge of the hallway. In its place were the stairs to the lower level.

"Come on," Soriya whispered as she took the first step.

The light from the stone guided them below, but it became unnecessary the moment they stepped out from the stairs to the floor proper. Recessed lighting took hold, coming to life with their arrival to the secret space.

"I don't think anyone has been down here in years." Soriya wiped away a thick cobweb hanging from the ceiling. She drifted through the contents. Shelves dominated the center. Workstations and research tables took up the far wall. Some texts sat in individual display cases; the books were opened but under glass for protection. Artifacts—rings, necklaces, and other charms—were held under lock and key in their own exhibits.

Soriya's companion's eyes widened as the room came into view. She glanced around, lost to the treasures of the past.

"These were too dangerous to hide with other artifacts from history," Soriya explained. Mentor had spoken of the place over the years. He had tried to impart as much of his wisdom as possible, but even Soriya found herself regularly in awe of the collection kept in the Vertrum home. "Too tempting a prize for those not worthy of the secrets."

Soriya was surprised at the caution the woman displayed. Her first instinct had always been to reach out, to explore with enthusiasm, never aware of the danger inherent with such secrets. The cloaked figure, however, seemed to know exactly the danger presented in the room even while caught up in the wonder of what surrounded her.

"These wardings…" she muttered. Her hand hovered over the protections coloring the front wall of the floor. They circled the perimeter of the home.

"They are meant to hide and to conceal what's inside," Soriya said. "I wouldn't touch them, or anything else."

The woman nodded. "It's… This is all… Magic."

"Potions, grimoires, wards, and more," Soriya confirmed. "Some date back centuries."

The woman hesitated in front of one of the opened texts kept under glass. The trim of the cover was golden and reflected the lights from overhead. "This… this is Egyptian."

Soriya joined her on the far side. "It was smuggled out of the Library of Alexandria before it burned."

The woman read through the pages. "It's talking about the rise of Thoth. No, about bringing Thoth back."

"Yeah," Soriya said, waving the woman away from the book. "Let's not read that one too closely. Thanks."

They traveled deeper into the room. Shelves took over, lined top to bottom with heavy tomes and handwritten archives. In the center of the room was an open workspace.

"What those women, and I use the term reluctantly, were throwing at us wasn't your standard energy bolts or elemental fire."

"No," the woman replied. "There was spellwork involved. Whispered incantations delivered faster than any I've ever encountered."

Soriya spun to face her companion. "Yet you recognized them as incantations."

"I'm not a witch," the woman shot back defensively. Soriya waited for more, and the woman sighed before removing her hood. "I explore the universe through the use of the spirit, and yes, that involves a level of magic, but—"

"You're not innocent in this, lady."

"I don't know what *this* is," the woman snapped. "And it's Annabelle. Any time *you* feel like sharing."

"Soriya," she answered. "And I have been. I didn't bring you here lightly."

"What the hell is your problem? What did I ever do—"

"The Minotaur," Soriya said. The woman's eyes flared with recognition, but she said nothing. "That ring a bell? He was what paid us a visit the first time you decided to open a door. He killed two cops."

"Two…"

"How about Shiva?" Soriya continued. "Remember that guy from the door at the docks? He killed hundreds and almost managed to take the rest of the city with him."

"I…" Annabelle paused with a hand to her trembling lips. "I didn't know. I wasn't trying to…"

"Yeah, well, those are on you."

"I'm… I'm sorry."

Soriya tried to hold her tongue. Apologies weren't going to cut it with her, but the argument was unnecessary. She turned away and caught a glimpse of what she had been looking for. She pushed past Annabelle and made a beeline for the book. It was one of Vertrum's manuscripts, those believed lost to time. Mentor had mentioned it in passing years earlier, though she had not made the connection until now.

"I recognized the spellwork they were using, too." Soriya pulled the book from the shelf. She was careful not to disturb the other items, knowing the possible danger should something fall loose.

"How?" Annabelle asked. "I barely did. The language they were throwing around hasn't been spoken in centuries."

"It was more than that," Soriya said as she paged through the text. "Their claim of sisterhood? The languages? Now where the hell is—" She carefully made her way deeper into the book. She scanned every page, every text piece, and every hand-drawn illustration until she reached what she had been searching for. "Here."

She moved for a clear table and placed the book down. Annabelle joined her, eyeing up the image and the scripted text on the opposite page.

"What is—"

She stopped when she made the connection as well. Soriya pointed it out all the same. It was the same image as the one hiding the first floor from view: the founders at the Vertrum home. Instead of the faded-out background, however, were the three women they had met earlier that night. The trio stood to the right of the gathering wearing the same green cloaks.

"They were here at the founding of Portents," Annabelle said. She turned to Soriya. "Who are they?"

"They call themselves the Daughters of Salem."

CHAPTER FOURTEEN

Mentor took his time wandering through the streets of Portents. There was no rush in his step, no pressing matters to attend to during his search for Soriya. He wanted her to succeed. More than anything, though, he wanted her to have fun with the game. Portents was their home, and the more she discovered on her own, the more effective she would become in her role as the Greystone.

He had given her all the tools she needed to be a positive force in the city. Soriya's eager mind had absorbed years of study and training—both physically and mentally. She was more than ready to take over for him, to be prepared for a time when he would no longer be there to help and guide her.

It was a day Mentor realized was getting closer with each breath. That was true for all, but he had seen his end. He had witnessed his demise at the hands of a killer with mismatched eyes and a hate that burned brighter than the stars. His death was coming, but Soriya would be ready. This was the next step to ensuring that goal.

Mentor stopped near the border of the red-light district and the Allure marketplace. There was a clear delineation from cobblestone road to pavement, from centuries-old architecture to the high-rises of downtown. Lamp light faded behind him while the hum of LEDs marked the path ahead.

The red-light district was always noise-ridden, a place of carnal delight that threatened the unspoken rules in Portents. The city wasn't safe at night, yet those who frequented the bars and clubs believed themselves impervious to the unwritten rules.

Perhaps what inspired their behavior was the lust for something more than the mundane. They sought out unnecessary risks for a chance to live on the edge if only for a moment. It was always a dangerous proposition to ignore the warnings in Portents. Tonight was no exception.

Mentor held tight to the edge of the Cobbler's Den. At first, he thought his knee was acting up. There was an ache from his old injury, yet that wasn't what was bothering him at all. It was a thrumming sound that reverberated up his body. He felt it along the brick of the building and through the soles of his well-worn sneakers on the cobblestone.

The sound built up like a wave, pounding through the earth and sending shocks in all directions. Mentor left the safety of the building and continued deeper into the downtown district. The sound grew with each footfall.

Blocks out from the first bar on the row, Mentor finally saw the source of the noise. Glass shattered on both sides of the road. Shards spread along the sidewalk and into the street. People leapt through the remnants, crying out into the night air like a pack of wild animals.

That was what they had become, though they held all the trappings of their everyday lives. Their clothes were ripped and torn, but still identifiable. Some wore shirts and ties as if just out of work, and the women kicked off heels as they bounded down the block.

Every soul that crashed out onto the street landed on all fours. They snarled at those around them. Fury filled their eyes, red like the burning embers of a flame. The creatures pushed at each other, trying to lay claim to the location.

Some ignored the territorial debate. They turned back to the bars, the stores, and the other establishments and jumped back inside. Screaming bystanders were tossed out into the warm night. They shouted both for their loved ones and for their very survival. For blocks this went on—as far as Mentor could see. Everything had gone straight to hell.

This wasn't the way the night was supposed to go. Mentor cursed under his breath at the change of plans. Tonight was supposed to be about having fun and enjoying the graduation of a woman who was like a daughter to him. It was meant to be about them, two souls sharing the joy of the city.

Portents had other ideas for them.

The game would have to wait. People were crying out for help; they begged for the darkness to abate and for a hand to reach out to save them. Mentor knew where he was truly needed.

He rushed into the fray without a thought for himself or the danger ahead. There was only the job because—for this one last night—*he* was the Greystone.

CHAPTER FIFTEEN

"That's all it says?" Annabelle asked.

"That's it, unfortunately," Soriya said. She read through the text again and tried to find some reason behind their return. Vertrum's notes did little to describe them beyond their unique origins. "The Daughters of Salem escaped the witch trials and joined a band of travelers who helped found the city."

Annabelle's brow furrowed. "Nearly two hundred years later. What about in between?"

She was right. The timing didn't line up. The Salem Witch Trials started in 1692. Dozens of women had stood accused and were summarily executed for their so-called crimes. These three had managed to escape their fate, yet hadn't turned up in the historical record again until after the American Civil War, when Portents was founded. Even if the daughters had survived the trials, as it seemed from Vertrum's narrative, they would have been dead and buried long before finding their way to Portents.

"Nothing." Soriya skimmed the pages of the book once more. "Nothing about their lives, their names, or what they were doing here. Just pictures of them with this guy."

Soriya passed along the book to Annabelle. She pointed to a series of images tucked into the folds. They were drawings of the three women. Vertrum appeared to have had quite the obsession with them, though he was never depicted with them. There was always someone else in the mix: a man with auburn locks and crimson eyes.

Annabelle studied the images. She picked one up and flipped it over for some indication of the subject. It merely read 'The

Daughters of Salem.' A black line smeared all other writing. It was the same on every picture. "His name has been removed completely."

Soriya didn't have an answer for her. She failed to recognize the man, though she felt she should have known him. He appeared to be important to the time period. His facial features matched those of the depictions of William Rath from the time, but the eyes were red instead of sky blue and his hair was auburn, not jet black. It was an almost insidious representation of the city's founder, especially compared to the heroic tales captured by Vertrum and so many others of the time.

"I thought there would be more," Soriya said.

"Story of my life," Annabelle muttered. It drew Soriya's curious gaze to her, and the cloaked woman waved down the eventual question. "Sorry. I know, you need to find a way to stop them, but for a second I thought there might be some answers here for me. Like what happened tonight was fated."

Soriya tried to hide a grin. She'd had her fill of fate and destiny. It had been a sticking point with another friend of hers—Kali, who was lost during their fight with the Raktabija. Just thinking about the strong-willed goddess caused Soriya's hand to drift to the ribbon snug against her left arm. She had been through so much over the last couple years and lost more than she would have thought possible. She couldn't let it happen again.

Annabelle ran her hands through her hair. Finding an empty slice of real estate along the wall, she slid to the floor and put her head between her knees.

"I was orphaned as a baby," she said, the words distant and lost to memory. "I bounced around foster homes, never able to find a place to belong. Never had a family. All I have of where I came from is here."

She lifted the sleeves of her cloak. Her arms were covered in tattoos. Glyphs and runes marked her pale skin in deep blacks. Soriya shifted closer for a better view.

"Those symbols..." Soriya trailed off. She knew them by heart.

"Cyrillic," Annabelle said as she pointed to one. "There's

Gothic and Vincan as well. I've tried to learn them all."

Soriya already had. They were some of her first lessons as a child. Most of the languages had disappeared centuries earlier, faded away like the people who had spoken them. Each, though, had been etched into the pillars surrounding the Bypass. The four pillars protected the floating orb at the center. They locked the energy within, controlling the crossroads to the infinite and containing the massive amount of power from exploding out into the city. Each one was somehow tied to the Bypass, and each symbol represented a secret no one should have known about, yet Annabelle had them on her skin.

Soriya said nothing, trying to hold back her questions. Annabelle never noticed; her eyes were firmly on the past and the tattoos.

"I thought if I learned everything about them I would find them... my parents. I could ask them who I am and where I belong." Annabelle swiped at her tired eyes. She shook her sleeves back down to cover the tattoos. "Sorry. That's probably not important. Not to you."

Soriya settled at her side. Her back leaned against the leg of the research table. "I lost my parents, too. There was a car accident when I was four."

Soriya had never shared much of the story about the blaze at Olcott Curve and the two figures killed in the crash. She had lost her very being that day, but had gained the stone in return. Everything about her life started over in the aftermath. Soriya never learned the truth about what had happened to her parents. Honestly, she never felt it was crucial to who she was meant to be. Mentor gave her a purpose, and she dove headfirst into her training.

Part of her, however, always returned to the fire. The loss of her past was like a weight tied to her ankle. Soriya reached out and took Annabelle's hand. "I understand the need for answers. But not at the expense of your life."

"I hoped to find them through the doors," Annabelle said. "It was wrong and selfish. I just needed to hear their voices and find a place for myself where everything made sense. It had to exist and if I could find it?"

Annabelle was clearly tortured by her failures. Three attempts had been made. Each had brought nothing but monsters and misery. This time, however, Soriya had been the reason for the failure.

Soriya let the woman's hand fall away, then stood. "You should get some rest. I'll keep looking for something we can use. There have to be some answers that might help."

"I could—"

Soriya shook her head. "You should rest while you can. This could take some time. If there are answers here, I'll find them."

Annabelle held out her hand, and Soriya helped her to her feet. "Thank you," the cloaked woman said. "For back at the shop. I didn't say it before, Soriya."

"Thank me when this is over," Soriya said. "I'll wake you if something comes up."

Annabelle nodded. She pointed to the darkness on the far side of the room. The corner appeared vacant of displays, yet it was secluded from the overhead lights. Soriya silently agreed, then watched Annabelle head off for a few hours of sleep.

Soriya hoped for some as well. Her eyes were bleary from the long night, but she required answers. She started back to the thick tomes for some secret or clue to unlock the puzzle the Daughters presented to Portents. She needed to find a way to stop them before something even worse happened.

CHAPTER SIXTEEN

Soriya was grateful for the solitude. She needed to figure out their next move. They couldn't remain at the Vertrum home, not with the Daughters of Salem hunting them. The sisters had somehow managed to track Annabelle to the Wiccan store, so there was no telling how quickly they would be able to locate the pair again.

They needed something from Annabelle. Her connection to the Bypass was clear. The tattoos on her arms tied her to the infinite crossroads. But as to the sisters' endgame, Soriya still had no clue.

The texts offered little in the way of clarity. For as much as Vertrum had documented the history of the city, he had fallen short in this regard. The Daughters were basically ghosts, hidden figures standing behind the prominent heads still honored by the citizens of Portents. What had their role been? Why had they come here of all places?

She'd encountered those questions many times before. With every threat, Soriya had looked into the reason behind their presence in her city out of all the hot spots in the world. Portents had been a magnet for trouble, and it would no doubt continue to be long into her role as Greystone.

Soriya quietly chuckled. She'd already taken to thinking of herself as the stone bearer, though her final test was still in progress. If Mentor had imagined how their fun game of hide-and-seek would turn out, what would he have said? What would he have done that she hadn't thought of?

The doubts were silly, of course. Mentor had struggled over

his career, the same as her. No one was perfect. She understood that now more than ever, but it no longer held her back. Her doubts no longer held sway over her actions. They merely drove her to be better, to do more if it was in her power.

Soriya sighed and took to the stairs. She left the confines of the first floor of the home for the publicly displayed portion of the tour. Soriya desired some fresh air and hoped to give Annabelle some time to rest.

Tonight was supposed to be a last hurrah for her as a student before graduating to the role of Greystone. Soriya held onto the past, though. She thought of Mentor and their lessons, almost wishing those lessons wouldn't end. Images of friends like Urg and Beth filtered through her mind and made her smile. She hoped things would never change.

Soriya stepped out on the landing of the home. The keypad continued to hang over the side of the metal railing. She attempted to put it back into place. Wires still dangled out, and it refused to sit flush with the wall. Soriya let it go. The box fell, swinging back and forth. It clanged against the metal, so she stopped the box in mid-air, resigned to the damage she'd caused by breaking into the place.

Rubbing at her eyes, Soriya tried to push away all thoughts of the past. Too much had been brought to the surface. Her parents. Mentor. Eddie. She needed to focus on the Daughters of Salem in the here and now.

Deep breaths helped her clear her mind. In the silence of her thoughts, Soriya woke to sounds in the distance. Her eyes scanned the block until she locked on the red-light district to the north. Lights flashed in the air, large beacons against the stark black clouds. Sirens blared, but they could not cover up the sound of screams—so many screams.

Soriya raced down the steps to the street. A fire erupted a few blocks away, and the explosive force drowned out everything else. Along the horizon a red mist sifted off the ground like a dust cloud.

The Daughters of Salem had been busy.

She should have seen it coming. It was always better to stand and fight rather than flee and regroup. She had been so concerned about Annabelle that she hadn't considered the danger to everyone else.

She couldn't let that stand. Soriya moved for the stairs and the slumbering woman inside. When she reached the door, which was still ajar from her departure, she hesitated. Annabelle was safe inside. She was hidden. There was nothing else for her to do in this situation.

This was Soriya's job to handle.

Soriya closed the door to the Vertrum home. She started for the screams in the distance, breaking into a run as soon as her sneakers hit the street. Unwilling to hide, Soriya raced headlong into danger.

CHAPTER SEVENTEEN

Eddie kicked at the workshop table. His foot collided with the leg of the metal bench, and he pulled back angrily at the stupid move.

Frustration had set in immediately after Soriya left. He didn't know why he had become so bothered by her visit, nor why he had felt the need to call her out about watching over of the shop and his work.

That wasn't quite true. He knew *exactly* why it had bothered him. Her keeping an eye on him had shown him the truth. For as much as he had pretended for the last year, as much as he'd tried to move forward with his life as Edward Smith, he remained Eddie Domingo at heart.

He had taken up refuge in the antique shop out of guilt for the death of Hephaestus. Guilt over past indiscretions did not equate rightful change or a true shift to good, though Eddie found the distinction incredibly naïve to begin with most of the time. He had tried to be good and do the right thing for those who frequented the shop. Did that make him a better person though? Or was he merely penitent for his wrongful deeds, hoping to do enough to wash away his past rather than accept both as part of his being?

Eddie held tight to the edge of the bench and sighed. The work could wait. Tonight had been nothing but a waste in terms of productivity; the visit from Soriya was the icing on the double-fudge-shit cake. He couldn't get the watch to work. Everything looked right, every component was set in perfect order, yet the watch refused to tick when activated. He'd stared at it for hours without success.

There was a simple solution to his problem. Hephaestus' hammer sat atop the bench just out of reach. One touch and his mind might open to the possible reasons for his failure. Eddie resisted, though. The hammer was a crutch, though he didn't mind it most of the time. But ever since Soriya stopped by, Eddie wanted to fix the watch on his own.

He wanted to stand on his own. He needed to prove to Soriya that he had changed, that there was some good in Eddie Domingo. Perhaps it was to prove to himself more than anyone else that his time at the shop had made him a better person. He knew he could change and be happy with life, unlike the pain of always living in fear of his family. He had grown, or tried to, yet felt nothing of the sort the second Soriya showed up.

"That's it," he grumbled. He dropped the watch to the bench and pushed it away. "This can wait until tomorrow."

Eddie clicked the light to the back room. His feet shuffled along the floor, and his toes still ached from kicking the workshop table. He paused at the entrance to the main shop and the exit to the street. Shelves remained stacked with completed projects. He had fixed them all, refurbished them, and—in some cases—completely overhauled the original item for a number of clients. He had done all of that. It was always with the hammer, of course, and never on his own.

Had *any* of it been him?

"Enough!" he shouted to the emptiness of the room. Eddie rubbed at his eyes and grabbed his coat from behind the counter. His keys jingled in his hand. Some sleep was in the cards, if only to silence his swirling thoughts.

Outside, a scream echoed in the air outside. He rounded the shelving units for a better look at the street and the usually peaceful marketplace.

"Help!" a woman yelled. She turned at the corner and raced by the storefront window. "Someone, please!"

Eddie blinked hard. "The kooks always come out at night," he commented as he moved for the door to the shop. "Must be a full moon or something."

The fleeing woman continued down the block, head cocked

to the side and eyes focused on the street behind her. Eddie tracked her frantic gaze.

A beast on all fours raced after her. Snarling growls boomed as the creature bounded in pursuit. Creature and beast were his first impressions, though they weren't quite accurate. The figure wore a shirt and tie, and its sports jacket shredded along the sleeves and collar. Expensive Italian shoes kicked at the pavement with each pounce.

"Okay," Eddie muttered. "Or something it is."

Eddie rushed through the store, throwing his coat on while juggling his keys as he moved. Coat secured and keys in his pocket, Eddie reached for the oversized hammer of his own creation resting against the counter. His hand clutched tight to the wooden hilt. He had promised Soriya that the tool had not been used for anything outside the occasional pest-control problem, but he wasn't about to take any chances.

"Eddie, what are you doing?" he asked himself as he stepped out on the street. "I wish I knew, brain. I wish to God I knew."

The woman was already at the end of the next block. The beast, however, closed the gap and grabbed for her. Eddie broke into a run with the hammer held out in front of him. It surprised him how easy it was to lift. His work might not have soothed his soul, but it had done wonders for his physique. That and the lack of late-night potato-chip-inspired binges on the couch with the newest video game certainly helped.

"Help!" the woman shouted once more. "Oh God, someone please help me!"

A claw snatched her shoulder. All momentum left her, and the woman fell back. The beast was on top of her a second later, slobbering over its potential victim.

"No, no, no, no…"

The beast's claw rose.

"Hey, buddy," Eddie called. "Personal space."

The beast shifted toward the voice. Eddie could see the creature fully now. It was a man, or had been a man, with wavy brown hair. His eyes were red, his teeth were sharpened to fangs, and his nails had grown to claws. Slobber ran down his lips. He looked like a rabid animal more than any kind of man

Eddie had ever seen before.

Eddie cocked the hammer back. "Damn, son. That's some overbite. Let me help you there."

He swung the hammer. The steel head slammed against the side of the beast, sending him soaring off his victim and through the window of a store across the street.

Eddie smiled. He lifted the hammer, proud of the weapon he had made with his own two hands. When he finished gloating in silence, he heard the muttered sobs of the woman at his feet.

He held out a hand for her. "Here."

"Thanks," she said as she worked her way slowly to her feet. She rubbed at her shoulder where the fabric of her shirt was torn away. "I can't even... He was..."

Behind them, the beast snarled. He smashed at the window display of the shop, tossing aside mannequins displaying seasonal wear.

Eddie grabbed the woman's hand. "Find the words later. I think your friend still wants a goodnight kiss."

He pulled at her, forcing her down the block toward the marketplace. She struggled to keep up with him, and both constantly peered back to the beast, who fought to escape the boutique.

"Where are we going?" she asked.

The beast reached the street and started after them. He closed the gap quickly. There was no way to outrun the creature. Eddie shifted from the open road ahead for the door of the antique shop. Knocking it open, Eddie pushed the woman inside.

"Get in!" he yelled. "Quick!"

With her secure in the shop, Eddie reached up and grabbed the security gate he'd installed when he'd taken ownership. He pulled down the mesh. It slammed to the ground, and he locked the gate in place. The beast was right outside, howling for blood.

Eddie hopped back into the store and shut the door. He dropped the hammer, grabbed the keys from his pocket, and jammed them into the lock to secure the store.

"Ha!" he said as he backed away from the glass. The beast clawed at the mesh. Pieces tore away with each swipe. He refused to stop, refused to even take a breath. His intentions were clear. He was not going away.

Eddie bumped into the shelving racks in the center of the store. He nearly jumped out of his skin at the collision. He tried to slow his heart when he caught the terror in the young woman's eyes.

"Hey there," he said in a soft voice. "It's okay now."

She offered a nod, unable to stop looking at the beast at the gate. "You saved me."

If only that were true. Eddie understood the reality of their situation, however. There was no exit to the back of the building—not even a window to slip through. The beast blocked the only door in and out of the shop.

"More like trapped us."

CHAPTER EIGHTEEN

Annabelle woke with a start. Her dreams had quickly turned to nightmares. Startling figures with horrifying faces had plagued her. She had been surrounded, unable to escape their torment. The Daughters of Salem haunted her. They demanded her power and ability. She could still hear their screams while she tried to shake the nightmares away.

The corner was dark. Tables, chairs, and smaller exhibits helped to block the overhead lights that had illuminated their entry to the secret space beneath the Vertrum home. Annabelle shifted along the wall. She rubbed at her eyes. It had been a long night, one that had spiraled so completely out of her control she could not help but wonder where she went wrong.

It was easy to discern. The truth of the matter was that her *entire plan* had been unsafe from the start. Annabelle had made two previous attempts only to be met with dismal results. Soriya had told her about the Minotaur's and Shiva's entry to the city thanks to the doors she had left unattended. Lives had been lost that she had been clueless about. Her focus had been solely on the family she continued to fail to find during her tireless search. She had never realized what Portents and Soriya had endured because of her actions.

Annabelle stood. Her legs ached from her awkward position in the corner of the room. She rubbed at her thighs and stretched to find a modicum of comfort. Stepping deeper into the confines of the secret room, Annabelle woke to the treasures surrounding her. She still couldn't believe places like this existed in the city. Despite all her searching and study, she had barely scratched the surface of possibilities.

She had been ignorant and continued to be so with every choice she made. Still, the wonders of the room soothed her battered ego. It was about more than her. It was about the threat unleashed—the Daughters of Salem. They had come for a reason and, unfortunately, it appeared to be centered on Annabelle.

The young woman chuckled. She wasn't anyone special in the grand scheme of things. She wasn't a power to be exploited or even important enough to be protected, though Soriya had done so without asking for anything in return. Annabelle wasn't anyone, not even to herself. She had always been a mystery, unable to recall her origins. She had been searching for her home for so long she had lost her way.

It reminded her of the Daughters in that regard. They had done everything, even sacrificed their own bodies, to return to the place they'd helped found more than a century earlier. A drop of envy swirled in her thoughts. They knew where they belonged and who they truly were, while the questions continued to plague Annabelle.

It was a sign of their strength. It gave them power. All her questioning did was make Annabelle weak. All her searching had done was cause pain and death. She had yet to deal with the ramifications of her actions. Instead, she ran from them just as she had from the Daughters of Salem. She should have fought them, should have found the strength to stand up to them like Soriya had.

Running was all Annabelle had ever done. She had fled from her failures with the first two doors, as well as from the foster homes and the families who had never bothered to understand her during her childhood. When would it end? When would she stop running? No answer came, and the silence of the room damned her weak soul.

"Soriya?" she called as she fought through her twisted thoughts. Her protector was nowhere in sight. Annabelle passed through the shelves full of texts. Each attracted her attention: the gold-trimmed for their opulence and the leather-bound editions for their age. Every text was unique and held knowledge beyond anything she could have imagined. They might have been the key to the questions she had asked since she was old enough to remember.

I wouldn't touch them, or anything else.

Soriya's warning kept Annabelle's hands at her sides and her mind cautious. She continued through the room until she reached the stairs. The paneling remained open at the second-floor landing. Annabelle climbed the steps and rounded the corner for the front door of the home.

"Soriya?"

There was no sign of her. Annabelle circled the property, then stepped outside. She scanned the area for some sign of the mysterious woman who had crashed into her life so suddenly. Soriya was gone, but where?

Fires raged in the distance. Flames rose from the fronts of clubs and bars that dominated the area. Screams echoed in the distance.

Annabelle's first instinct was to run. That had always been her immediate reaction to conflict. Let it be someone else's problem. That was how she had always handled life when it became too difficult. This time was different, however. Annabelle knew the truth behind the chaos unfolding in the city—and she knew exactly where Soriya had gone.

Soriya was facing the horror head on. She was using the courage and strength inherent in her every act to tackle the problems plaguing Portents. They were problems Annabelle had created through her misguided efforts.

Annabelle took a deep breath. This was her fault. She had to take a stand. She scurried down the steps to the street, then headed deeper into the downtown area. It was time to make things right.

CHAPTER NINETEEN

The monsters had the run of Club Noir. They controlled the streets, grabbing at anyone panicked enough to try to escape. They snarled at each other more than their victims as they fought for each piece of flesh and the pleasure of each kill.

It was Mentor's fifth stop of the night. He had been fighting his way up the block for over an hour. He'd struggled to make headway against the stream of creatures that had taken hold of the area. Creatures had been a misnomer, one he'd learned immediately upon engaging them. They were human, or had been at one point. Something had changed them. It had taken their common decency and twisted it to a bloodlust unlike any the aging teacher had ever seen.

His first few stops had done little to stop the conflagration. There was violence, but in each case the odds had been on his side. He had beaten the beasts down and carried on without looking back.

Club Noir was much worse. Instead of one infected person there were multiple, the crowd much denser inside. Mentor dove into the fight, though he already felt the pain rushing up his right leg. Stamina had been in short supply ever since his battle with the Minotaur, but he pushed through the growing pain to protect those in need.

Mentor grabbed hold of one of the monsters lingering outside the club and wrapped his arm around the beast's throat. He pulled the creature clear of its intended victim, while holding tight to cut off the monster's air supply. *Not a monster*, Mentor tried to remind himself when he noticed the woman's outfit and

the ticking watch on her wrist. Taking into account their inno-
cence in the night's events was tricky, but Mentor did his best to
make sure none suffered any lasting injuries.

Unfortunately, they weren't giving him the same luxury. As
Mentor let go of the woman, who crumpled unconscious to the
pavement, another slashed at his back. Mentor cried out and
quickly fell away before a follow-up blow sliced him further. He
spun around to face his foe, this time a man. The beast launched
at Mentor. Fully committed to the strike, the creature was wide
open, so Mentor used it to his advantage. He side-stepped the
blow, then slammed down on the man's back to drive him to
the ground. A swift kick snapped the man's head viciously to the
left, and the beast collapsed at Mentor's feet.

The others scattered in Mentor's presence. Their attention
had been drawn away while Mentor took care of the first two.
They chased after the innocents who were looking to escape
from the clubs and bars dominating the strip. Mentor started for
the closest, before he heard the cries from inside Club Noir.

He hesitated. There were too many threats and too many
people in danger. Mentor shook his head to wipe away his
doubts, then raced for the club entrance.

Club Noir was in ruins. Music continued to blast through the
jukebox, though the sound was garbled from broken and battered speakers. People screamed. They hid behind overturned
tables or huddled together in the corners. Beasts snarled at little
outcroppings of innocents, ready to strike.

Mentor's foot slammed into the nearest threat's knee. The
beast howled and fell. As it did, Mentor slammed his fist into its
jaw. He didn't bother to wait before he moved to the next. Behind him, people fled to escape the club.

Two others remained trapped in the back corner. The young
man and woman hugged tight to the wall at their back. Panic
filled their eyes, and they were unable to look away from the
man growling at them. He wore a plaid button-down and khakis,
both of which had seen better days.

"Phil?" the woman cried. Her hands were in front of her to
defend herself. "Phil!"

The beast's claw rose. When it came down, Mentor jumped

in front of the others. He blocked the blow and drove the arm away. His counterstrike, a kick to the gut, sent the beast over the closest table.

Mentor turned to the pair in the corner. "You need to move. Now."

"I can't," the woman said. She pointed to the creature, who chewed through the table in anger. "I can't leave him like this. He's… he's…"

Mentor's hands fell to her shoulders. He blocked her view of the monster. "What happened?"

"He was fine," she replied. "We were dancing, and then—"

The man at her side knocked Mentor's hand away, then pulled at the woman. "What did you do, Grace? Did you say something to Phil?"

Grace looked aghast. "Did I say something to turn him into a cannibalistic monster? Christ, Wes."

"What?" Wes exclaimed. "I'm freaking out!"

Mentor sighed. "Do you two mind heading for the exit?"

Grace shook her head. "Not without—"

Phil was back on his feet. The creature snarled at them. He gnashed his teeth, slobber running down his chin. When he was on all fours, he barely even appeared human, with deep red eyes as well as thick claws.

Grace glanced at him. Terror filled her face when she turned back to Mentor. "Okay. We'll leave."

"Good," Mentor said. He dove for the creature as the pair fled for the street. Knocking Phil back to the ground, Mentor used his momentum to roll clear. He bounded back to his feet to follow the pair.

Wes pulled at Grace to keep her moving. "I was just thinking that… maybe if you had been nicer to him, maybe this wouldn't have happened."

"Shut. Up. Wes." Grace pinched his arm.

"Ow!" he shouted, holding the 'wound.' "Okay! Shutting up."

More joined their flock as they fled for the front of the club. Mentor kept things orderly while leading the charge. Flames flickered around them; the chaos from the struggle had ignited spilled alcohol and damp cloths.

Before they could reach the front door, one of the support beams above collapsed. Mentor held up the line of panicked patrons. They rushed against his efforts, unable to see in the cloud of smoke rising from the falling debris.

The way out was blocked.

"What do we do now?" one yelled. The sentiment was echoed by the others in turn. Mentor scanned the room. The beasts at their back were regrouping and ready for blood.

Reaching for his hip, Mentor removed the Greystone from the hand-woven pouch tied to his belt.

As he channeled his will into the stone, air swirled before him. The elements answered his call, and a gale force streamed forth. It lifted the beam from the ground and knocked it clear of the exit. Just as quickly as it had begun, the wind died down. The light from outside filled the entry, and Mentor pointed ahead.

"Everyone to the streets!"

People flooded the street. Some ran left, others fled to the right, all in the hopes of avoiding the monsters among them. Mentor stayed with the stragglers. Grace and Wes helped lead a small group. They had made it halfway down the block before the flashing lights of a squad car filled the air.

The car came to a screeching halt, and the pair of officers within rushed out. The driver's hand hovered over his service weapon as he approached Mentor.

"What the hell is going on here?"

The shattering of windows answered him. Creatures came from both sides, crashing into the street. The cops grabbed for their guns.

"Don't shoot," Mentor said. He crept closer until he was next to the driver. His fingers gently gripped the barrel of the officer's sidearm and lowered it. Mentor ushered the wounded from Club Noir toward the police cruiser. "I need you to escort these people to safety."

"We will, sir," the young man in uniform answered. "Just as soon as we take care of this. So step back and let us handle this. Right, Stu?"

There was no response from the other side of the vehicle. The officer peered over the squad car for signs of his partner. Stu lay on the ground. Slash marks ran across his neck, and a stream of blood trailed from his body to the beast at his side.

"Stu?"

Mentor and his companions recognized the monster as Phil. Grace's hand fell over her lips. She tried to look away from the carnage, but couldn't.

"I'm glad I never slept with him."

Wes grimaced. "You're so conceited."

"You were thinking it, too!" she shot back.

He sighed. "Yeah. I was."

Mentor grabbed the lone cop by the collar. He snapped his fingers to try to keep the man from going into shock. The young officer shook his head and blinked rapidly.

"Officer," Mentor said. "These people need a safe way out. I need you to lead them away from here as quickly as you can. I will cover you."

"But—"

Mentor let him go. "Do it now. Please."

The officer nodded. His hands gripped tight to his sidearm. "Okay, people. Let's move!" They rushed past him for the darkness down the block. Before joining them, the cop paused. "Are you sure you're—"

"I'll be fine," Mentor said. The group fled for the shadows. Satisfied at their distance from the struggle, Mentor turned his attention back to the street. The transformed men and women of Portents gathered before him. They snarled and growled for his blood. Mentor reached for the Greystone. "I'll hold them off for as long as I can."

CHAPTER TWENTY

The world disappeared. Everything faded to red for Urg. Every rational thought, every fear and doubt, was suppressed by a driving need. There was only a single goal for him: chaos. It was a hunger. The sensation sat in his gut. The need pulsed through his body, pounding in his chest and in his mind.

The change had come suddenly. The red mist had been in the air, a gift from the floating women and their devilish grins. The red had surrounded him, and everything had suddenly shifted for the mountainous orc. He fell to all fours. His cry turned to a snarl, then shifted to a growl. The spikes that dominated his neck and shoulders grew. They sliced through the fabric of his Stafford button down and right through his suit jacket as if it was paper. His nails sharpened and spread from the tips of his fingers into claws. They dug into the pavement in long slashes.

Anything human about him, from his manner of dress to the accent he'd cultivated during his decades in the city, vanished. What had made Urg unique was squashed for the purposes of the twisted sisters, who continued their travels deeper into the district.

He needed no further instruction. Prodding was unnecessary. Everything had been intuited by the shift. His animal side took over. Every instinct was heightened. Every scent, sight, and sound was more immersive and layered than it had been before. So much had been lost in translation when his mind was in charge of processing sensory information. Now, everything was pure—undiluted by conscience or morality—thanks to the loss of all humanity.

All that remained was the desire implanted within him by the witches. It was a need to rip everyone in sight apart. He wanted nothing more than to bathe in their blood, tear their flesh with his claws, and feed on their bones. The very thought caused his growls to turn to howls of delight.

Behind him, Night Owls was in a panic. Patrons screamed for a way out. They begged for a path back to the normality that had been stripped from them in an instant. Only moments earlier, their only concerns had been centered on liquor and companionship. Their only care had been on the next song from the jukebox or whose turn it was for darts.

Four of the patrons in the bar joined Urg in the change. They growled in ecstasy at the loss of their human shells. Everyone around them fled, only to be blocked by Urg. Some took to the windows, shattering the glass with bar stools.

When they reached the street, they scattered. The beasts inside the club followed suit to prey on the weakest of the bunch. Urg hesitated. He scanned the crowd for the right victim—the one to sate the ravenous desire that dominated his every thought.

He found her in front of the club. The heels of her knee-high boots crunched the glass scattered from the window. Her hands stretched for those wounded in the initial burst of violence. She helped them escape the club for the street.

"It's okay," she said, her voice loud enough to carry over the screams of the others down the block. She tried to calm them and distract those hurting from their surroundings. Urg's brethren had already begun their first feast of the night. "Take my hand. Come on."

Urg growled at her from the front door of the club. Drool collected along his lips and ran down the fangs still growing in his mouth.

"Hurry. Come on," the woman in the jean skirt said. She pulled at another pair still inside. They struggled over the glass, knocking away a few of the remnants as they fell to the sidewalk.

Urg approached slowly. The red took over. All he saw was

his victim.

"Run," she said without looking at the others. She cut off Urg's approach to give them a moment to escape. "Run now!"

He didn't care. *She* was the one he was after, the one he had planned for the moment his world turned red.

The woman held her hands before her. "Urg. This isn't you. Don't—"

He lunged at her. She ducked to the side, and he crashed into the scattered glass, slipping down the pavement. The sharp edges perforated the shredded clothing and scraped his rock-hard skin.

She ran in the opposite direction of the chaos. Urg was on her a second later. All her strength faded the second he grabbed her shoulder and pulled her to the ground. She kicked at the pavement for some distance. He snatched her ankle, and his claws dug through her boot into her skin. She cried out, which only caused his excitement to rise even more.

Urg pulled her closer to his salivating fangs. He was ravenous, lost to the red. Her death was all he could think of and all he wanted.

CHAPTER TWENTY-ONE

All thought left Soriya. There was no need for pondering, no question about the action in front of her. People were being hurt, they were in danger, and she was the only hope for them.

Soriya raced into the fray of the red-light district. The obsidian tower cast a darkness over the area, but even in the dim haze of street lamps and the sparking blazes throughout the area, Soriya could see the red mist rising from the ground.

What the strange phenomenon meant escaped her. It was like a riot had broken out suddenly. There was no rhyme or reason behind the wave of violence that had erupted in the six-block radius. The riot was concentrated on that single area and had caused the men and women trapped within to lose their grip on sanity. Or so it appeared to the young woman who rushed to their aid.

It wasn't until she was close enough that Soriya noticed the beasts among them. Snarls for blood filled the air from the creatures hunched on all fours. They leapt at the fleeing men and women who were trying with all their might to escape the bar scene.

The monsters were unrecognizable to the young woman at first. One wore a blue dress and broken heels. Her fangs snapped at a cowering man pressed tight to the brick exterior of a night club. Before the beast could reach its intended victim, Soriya jumped between them. She landed a swift kick to its face that sent the creature to the ground.

She turned to the terrified man and pointed for the shadows of uptown. "Go! Get out of here!"

"N-no… I can't," the man stammered. He shook his head. "You don't understand."

"What? What don't I understand?" Soriya asked, eyebrow cocked in curiosity. "That this thing wants you for a meal?"

"That… Oh God," the man said with tears running from his eyes. He ran his hands through his hair.

The beast was back on its feet. It jumped at Soriya, but she was ready. The stone bearer slammed her fist against the creature's cheek. Unwilling to allow it to get back up, Soriya followed the blow to where the beast landed and battered it with a series of kicks to make sure it stayed down.

"Stop!" the man shouted from behind her. "Please! You have to stop!"

Soriya shifted back to the man. He pushed from the wall in a struggle to stay upright. Soriya reached out to keep him from falling.

"What is it?"

"That's my…" His eyes widened. "That's my wife!"

As she glanced around the block, the situation became clear to Soriya at last. The creatures wore the trappings of humanity. They shared the same form. They were humans, who had been twisted and turned into monsters.

"Oh," she said. Soriya wiped the blood adorning her knuckles along her jeans. "Counseling didn't work out, did it?"

"What are you—?"

"It's called levity," Soriya said. "It's all I've got at the moment."

His wife growled behind them. Both turned to face the creature. Soriya let the man loose, fists clenched tight before her.

"You need to run," Soriya told him.

He shook his head profusely, even as the creature moved closer. "My wife…"

"She isn't answering your calls right now," Soriya snapped. She pushed at him. "Go!"

He hesitated a brief moment. A loving gaze fell on his wife. When she bellowed back at him with the howl of an animal, he finally snapped out of his delusion. Love shifted to terror, and he ran.

The beast pursued, but Soriya cut off the transformed wife. The ribbon of Kali slid down her arm and shot forward. A strand latched tight to the creature's arm. Snapping to the left, the tense fabric sent the beast soaring through the shattered window of the nearby night club. Crashing sounds erupted from within as tables broke from the impact.

Soriya peered into the club. The woman lay among the rubble, unconscious. The ribbon retracted, then slid back up Soriya's arm as if it contained a will of its own.

"One down," Soriya muttered. The block stretched out before her. Six more creatures waited for her. Their attention must have been drawn by the sudden resistance. Soriya readied for the fight, but her every thought tried to understand the chaos and the purpose behind it.

The Daughters of Salem were behind this. There was no question about that in her eyes. "But why?" she asked to no one present. "What does this madness give you?"

Her fists dropped, and her attention was pulled from the threat ahead to the danger left behind. Soriya looked toward the Vertrum home as the answer slammed into her.

"Oh hell," she said. "All this chaos? It gives you me. Out here. Away from…"

Annabelle. She had done everything she could to keep the doormaker safe. It had been to protect her, while also preventing the Daughters from achieving their dark intentions. And now she had left Annabelle unguarded.

The beasts growled for her attention. They encircled her, trying to lock her into a fight she couldn't face—not if it cost Annabelle her safety. The doormaker had to be the priority.

As they crept ever closer to her, Soriya loosed the ribbon of Kali once more. It was not to strike back or attack, as had been her initial intention. No, the people of the district would have to fend for themselves for the moment. The fight here was nothing more than a distraction to draw Soriya away from the actual threat.

The ribbon snapped upward. It latched onto the streetlight hanging over the corner and wrapped tight. The ribbon pulled taut. When the first beast launched at her, fangs wide and salivating with anticipation, Soriya felt her feet leave the ground.

She flew into the air. Hands grabbed the streetlight, and she swung clear of the fight. The moment she landed back on the street outside the circle of monsters, Soriya ran away. The ribbon was quick to return to its place on her left arm.

She hated to do it, hated to flee when every instinct in her body demanded the fight. However, there was no choice in the matter. Annabelle was the priority; she was the true target of the three witches inflicting such pain on Portents.

The Vertrum home wasn't far, and at a full run Soriya reached the front door on the second level within minutes. She was through the main corridor and down the hidden staircase seconds later.

"Annabelle?" she called from the base of the steps. "Annabelle, where are you?"

There were no signs of life in the secret repository. Soriya journeyed deeper through the tome-filled shelves and display cases. Each step was more hurried than the last. Her breath caught in her throat when she reached Annabelle's resting spot. The corner was vacant. Annabelle was gone.

What have I done?

CHAPTER TWENTY-TWO

Nothing was familiar, and nothing helped Annabelle find her way through the city. Every city block seemed strange and unknown. The cold added to her discomfort, so she hugged her arms tight to her sides. The thick hood hid stray locks of scarlet from view as well as her growing fear.

Blocks passed. Her pace increased with each street left behind. She journeyed north, then south, winding like a snake through the city. Her fears gave way to doubts, and she hesitated to proceed. She wanted to run and hide. More than anything, she wanted someone else to be brave for her and stand in her place.

There was no one else around for her, though. Homes were closed up, their lights off to enjoy the silence of the night. Annabelle was on her own. She pushed through her doubts. She had ventured out to help and had to see it through. She passed through residential neighborhoods before returning to the businesses of downtown.

The red-light district was aglow. Blazes lined the outskirts, and a red haze rose from the street. Screams filled the air. Chaos held the area in its grip, driving folks from the bars and night clubs in a panic.

What happened here?

The monsters came into view. They wore shirts and ties, skirts and heels.

People. They're people.

"I did this." The cause had been clear from the start. The red mist alone clued the woman in to the root of the problem. They were herbs and potions she had kept at her shop.

This was all her fault. She might not have unleashed the magic on the people in the district, but she had put the ingredients together. She had kept them out in the open for anyone to purchase or—in the case of the Daughters of Salem—steal.

Annabelle had brought the Daughters to the city. Soriya may have interrupted her spell, but it had been Annabelle's efforts that created the potential for the nightmare.

Hell, even without the interruption there had been no guarantee of success. She was no closer to finding her home or learning the truth about her family and where she had come from. Years of research, of endless study, had given her nothing but disaster.

It was all because of magic. The potential power through one's pure will had always intrigued her. Her fascination had started because of the runes tattooed to her skin. They were birthmarks she had carried her entire life, like a genetic link to her true family. Unfortunately, Annabelle's study of magic had always separated her from the world. It had caused her to be bounced from foster home to foster home. They had feared the power in her, the potential danger of her studies, and her inherent talent.

The Daughters, however, savored her power and desired her potential. They wanted to unleash it on the city. The chaos of the red-light district was just a taste of their plans. In a single act, the trio of witches had brought the area to its knees. They were destroying Portents from within.

Sobs snapped Annabelle from her thoughts. She had been locked in place for minutes, staring out at the danger running rampant through the streets. She shook off the shock of the scene and moved for the sound of the weeping. A woman cowered in the shadows of a nearby alley. She hid behind a dumpster with terror in her eyes.

A creature surveyed the block. Once a man in a faded t-shirt and shorts, the beast sniffed the air for potential victims. Annabelle tucked close to the building. The green cloak helped her blend in with the shadows. When the creature turned in the opposite direction, the young woman rushed into the alley.

"Ma'am?" Annabelle whispered. She shuffled to the far side of the dumpster. "Are you okay?"

The woman kept her distance from Annabelle. She shook her head. "He's..." the woman started. Her hands were shaking, and she fought to keep them contained in her lap. "He turned into something else. A monster. I... I don't know how... I don't know where to go."

"I can help," Annabelle said. She reached for the woman. When she stretched forward, the sleeve of her cloak pulled back, and the woman caught a glimpse of the runes adorning Annabelle's skin.

The woman reeled back and batted the hand away. "No! You could be one, too!"

"I'm not," Annabelle said. She kept her voice calm. Sadness crept in, though, at the horror on the woman's face. "I want to help. Please..."

The woman slapped at the air between them. She rounded the dumpster, backing up toward the street. "Get away from me!"

"Don't," Annabelle whispered. "Don't do—"

The woman reached the street, yet she barely lasted two seconds before a shadow fell over her. The beast was back. In the blink of an eye, the woman was gone—another victim of Annabelle's mistake.

Annabelle fell to the ground behind the dumpster. Sobs wracked her body. "I'm sorry. I'm so sorry."

She didn't know how much time had passed before she found the strength to leave the alley. The beasts had moved farther down the district. The closest flames were now only a flicker compared to the devastation down the way. The screams fell into the background. The snarls and growls of the monsters joined the chorus as she stared at the destruction caused by her actions.

"This is all my fault."

There was nothing she could do, and no help she could offer. She had been a fool to believe she had the same strength as Soriya. Annabelle was no protector. She could do little but get in the way of Soriya's efforts to keep everyone safe.

It was time to go. Annabelle fled for the shadows. The city fought against her. It offered her no refuge in the night. Everywhere she turned was emptiness. Blocks disappeared under the pounding of her shoes on the pavement, until she simply collapsed on the street. Her hands covered her face, and she cried in despair.

"I've made such a mess of everything."

"Then help us fix it, child," a voice replied.

Annabelle's hands fell away. Despair turned to utter terror as the Daughters of Salem hovered before her. "Oh, no."

'Fix it all!' Maggie's mental cry shouted. Annabelle moved to cover her ears, then stopped, knowing it would make no difference. *'Fix us. Fix the city.'*

"Stay back," Annabelle said. "I'll—"

"—do nothing," the eyeless witch said with a sneer. "Too untrained. Too weak."

Mercy held out her hand. "Time to come home, child. Time for all of us to set things right. Together."

'Family,' Maggie bellowed through her mind.

Mercy closed in on Annabelle, who was frozen in terror. "Yes, Sister. One big, happy family."

CHAPTER TWENTY-THREE

The monster was at the gate. Literally.

Eddie tried not to peer toward the front of the shop. Shifting behind the shelving units in the center of the store helped block the snarling menace from view. He kept his focus on the woman next to him instead.

She was gorgeous. In the rush of adrenaline during the fight in the street and the race back to the shop for safety, Eddie had failed to notice much about her other than her gender. Now, he couldn't look away. She was young, early 20s was his impression. Purple highlights ran down one side of her thick brown hair. She was shorter than him by a few inches, with rosy cheeks and a lean figure. Her hands fidgeted in front of her as she paced through the shop.

"This can't be happening," she muttered beneath her breath. "This can't be happening."

Eddie gave her some distance in the hopes that she would work through the shock of the night. He sure as hell didn't have a clue what to say to calm her nerves. Pulling her purse strap tight to her shoulder, the woman rounded the shelving units. The monster slashed the security gate with renewed zeal when he caught sight of her. She immediately retreated behind the units.

"Okay," she said, finally able to look at him. "So this is really happening."

A flicker of a smile escaped Eddie. Even the sound of her voice was lyrical to his ears. He lowered his hammer against the counter.

"Hey," he said. When he reached for her shoulders, she flinched. "You're okay." His eyes widened, and he took a step away from her. "Wait. Are you okay? I didn't think to check you out. I mean, check you over…"

Eddie huffed, and the woman smirked at his embarrassment. He let out a long breath, hands falling to his hips.

"I mean look for wounds. Obviously."

"I'm fine," she replied.

"Good," Eddie said. He pointed toward the door without looking. The sound of shattering metal boomed through the store. "So who the hell is that guy?"

Her head lowered, and she bit her lower lip near the piercing along the left side. "The day trader."

"What?"

She sighed. "He works in stocks. Only guy who comes into the bar where I work wearing suits that cost more than I make in tips in a year. He was watching the basketball highlights like he always does. Then…" She stopped and turned toward the door.

Eddie blocked her view of the beast outside. "Hey. We're safe here."

He knew it was a lie. The store was old, much too old to conform to modern-day safety requirements. The previous owner, Hephaestus, had blocked off the store's other point of egress to complete his workshop in the back. Now there was only the front door. It was their only way in and, unfortunately, their only way out of the mess Eddie had managed to get them into thanks to his less-than-stellar quick thinking. He never should have said anything before, but he had always found clamming up to be one of his bigger weaknesses.

Thankfully, the woman was more focused on her story. "He killed people," she said. Her eyes flared in panic, a hand to her lips. "And the others? My friends at the bar? I ran. I never even looked back. What if they—"

She started for the door. Eddie knocked her hand from the knob. "Hold it!"

"They might need me."

"To do what?" Eddie asked. He kept his hand over the knob

to make sure the lock was still in place. "Die? You open the gate and that guy will gut you in seconds."

Her lips quivered. Slowly, she backed away. Tears filled her eyes. "Which one?"

"What?"

With shaking fingers, she pointed outside. "There's two now."

Eddie turned, then took a step from the door. She was right. During their argument, another well-dressed, slobbering beast had joined the day trader. The newcomer was male as well, and his suit was nothing but tatters. Both clawed at the gate, causing it to shake.

Eddie took the woman by the hand. He pulled her toward the back of the shop. They left the storefront behind, heading for the darkness of the storage area and then to the workshop.

At the threshold of the dimly lit space, the woman stopped. "We're not safe here, are we. Not really."

"We'll... We'll be fine. The gate will..." Eddie waved her forward. She took a step into the room, and he threw the door shut. "We'll be fine."

The sound of breaking metal and the snarls of the monsters at the gate faded into the background. Neither needed the constant reminder of what was coming.

Still, the woman shook with fear. She slipped off her purse and slammed it against the workbench in the center of the room. Then she sniffled back the onslaught of tears as she held tight to the edge of the wooden work space.

"We're going to die," she said. Her words were shaky and quiet. "I can't believe I was so stupid. Taking a job bartending at night? In this town?"

Eddie sidled next to her. "The gate might hold."

"Why are you so calm?"

He nearly laughed. "I'm not."

Every fault and every poor decision passed through his spinning thoughts. From his time with the Domingo family, to the robbery that ended the life of Hephaestus, to his stupid pride when it came to Soriya's visit earlier that night, his every action had been flawed from inception to execution. It was *his* fault they were trapped in the shop.

"I could have taken you anywhere," he said with mounting frustration. He pushed from the bench, fists clenched in front of him. "There are a dozen safer places less than a mile from here. Even the damn precinct isn't that far. But I brought you here. And you talk about stupid."

"What do you—"

"This?" he snapped. He showcased the room, then pounded his chest in anger. "This isn't me. What the hell was I thinking? I don't know what to do, how to help people. I pretend. I'm a *damn* good pretender, but when the chips are down? My hands won't stop shaking. I can't see a way out. And that gate?"

"It might hold," she said, foolish hope in her eyes. "You said—"

"I lied, lady!" Eddie shouted. "I trapped us in here like a fool."

Eddie covered his face and screamed into his palms. He closed his eyes, trying to calm his nerves. His hands shifted up and through his hair.

When his eyes opened, the woman was before him. "Hey."

Eddie shook his head. "I killed you."

Her hand dug into his arm. "You saved me. You went out there and rescued me."

The beast would have killed her. There was no doubt about its intentions. Eddie hadn't needed to go out, he hadn't needed to act on the behalf of another. He could have ignored the world, as he had done for so many years during his former life. He could have looked out only for himself. Instead, he'd focused on the well-being of another.

"I did that?"

"You did," she said. The curl of her lips caused a small dimple to form on her cheek.

Eddie stood taller. He had put someone else's needs ahead of his own. He had saved someone. For all his doubts, Eddie *had* been doing better and had changed since his time with the Domingos. He was a better person, just like Soriya believed him to be.

With renewed confidence, Eddie moved for the door. "Lock

the door after I leave."

"Where are you going?" she asked. Her terror quickly returned. "You can't go out there. They'll kill you."

Eddie smiled. He pulled her close. Comforting hands ran up and down her arms. "Trust me." He waited for her chest to stop heaving and for the panic to fade. "Lock the door. Barricade it. You'll be safe."

"And you?"

"I'll be all right," he said as he let her go. Eddie stepped into the darkness. He was barely a foot away when the door slammed shut and the lock clicked into place. Eddie reached the storefront, the streetlight outside beaming across the stocked shelves.

The two beasts howled at his arrival. They clawed at the gate for all they were worth. Eddie grabbed the hammer from the counter and clutched it tight.

"I hope."

CHAPTER TWENTY-FOUR

Urg pulled his victim closer. The woman kicked with her free leg, swinging wildly as she clawed at the pavement. She tried to get loose. She tried to knock him aside and escape. It wasn't going to happen.

Every instinct demanded her death. He could already taste her entrails. He could hear her delicious screams of agony as he tore her apart piece by piece. His anticipation grew with each passing second. He held onto it as tightly as he did his victim, wanting to savor every shred of terror that flew from her lips. The sensation completed him.

"Please," she yelled. "Urg! You don't have to do this!"

He didn't recognize the name, and he barely heard her pleas through the red haze of the witches' brew. The mist had taken every restraint, every last shred of humanity from the centuries-old orc. All that was left was his animal side—the one that hungered for blood.

The victim was a blur as well. She was merely what he needed at the moment. His desire for slaughter outweighed everything else.

Blood smeared the street. Her nails cracked and broke from her struggling. Still, he pulled her closer. Every second her screams intensified was music to Urg's blissful ears.

"Oh, God," she pleaded. "Please…"

He tore at her skirt. His nails scraped along her skin. Each swipe sent tears flooding from her eyes like a tidal wave. Nothing gave him pause, and nothing made him hesitate. The beast in him needed more. The red demanded it.

"This…" her voice cracked from the strain. She was so close to him. His breath wafted over her body. "This isn't you, Urg. This isn't who you are."

He didn't know *who* he was. He didn't care to know who he was. Nothing mattered beyond her death. There wasn't a single thought beyond the sweet chaos her murder would create and the immense pleasure that would fill him. That was his only imperative.

"You have to listen to me, Urg," she said. "It's me, Rachel. You don't want to do this. You don't have to do this. Let me go. Let it all go."

She stared at him, begging to be heard. Her hand reached for him. Through her words, and the power of her resistance, Urg saw her at last. It was not Rachel, the friend he had come to love and respect over the years. Not *just* her, at any rate. Urg saw someone else through the haze of the red mist.

Soriya.

He saw her not only as she was, but as she had always been. He recalled the time they had first met when she was only seven. He could see the smile that had been on her face at the sight of him, so strong and unafraid at the strange green-skinned behemoth walking in the rain. In that split second of recognition he heard her voice in his head, and he heard all the dreams she'd told him, those he had held for her thanks to their shared friendship. All became intermixed with the red. They drowned out the incessant call for blood.

In seeing Soriya through the eyes of Rachel, Urg drew back. His grip slackened along her leg, and he stopped pulling her.

Rachel seized the opportunity and kicked out at her attacker. Her foot collided with his face. Over and over, she slammed her heel against him. She bit back her fear and fought for her freedom. "Let. Go. Now."

Urg fell away, driven to his side by her blows. Rachel pushed off from the street to get some distance from the beast. Urg rubbed at the stream of blood running down his cheek.

Rachel fought for her feet, shuffling farther and farther away from him. Tears continued to stream from swollen eyes. Her bleeding fingers wrapped tight before her as she staggered away from her attacker.

Urg called out to her, "Wait…"

Night returned. The red receded from his view. When he held his hand before his eyes, he noticed the claws fading and his nails beginning to take shape once more. The snarls and growls that had dominated his speech shifted to language, though it felt so distant he wasn't quite sure it had come from him.

"I didn't mean…" he said. Rachel didn't look back. She ducked down the closest alley for shelter. "Rachel, I…"

With the red gone, every instinct disappeared. Every imperative to hunt and maim and destroy faded like it had never been there. The world came back into view.

Urg rolled to his back, then sat up. A groan fell from his lips. His head felt like it was ready to burst, worse than any hangover he had ever endured. There had been quite a few of those in his lifetime.

He stared at his hands, no longer shaped into claws. He felt his arms up to his shoulders. The spikes had returned to normal, though the damage had been done to his suit. There was barely enough left to call it a jacket. The tatters whipped along the breeze, threatening to peel away completely with the slightest pull. He finished the job started by his transformation. The jacket tore in two, and he tossed the pieces aside in frustration. Loosening his tie, he watched the wind pick it up and send it swirling behind him.

"Someone is going to pay for this," he grumbled as he stood. Chaos continued to unfold down the block. Monsters, twisted by the red mist, pulled innocents from the bars and dragged them down the street. Violence raged all around him. Dozens screamed for help. Urg took a sharp breath, then moved to lend a hand.

CHAPTER TWENTY-FIVE

"Not another step!"

Soriya found them north of Redmond. Annabelle knelt in the middle of the street as the Daughters of Salem closed in around her. Mercy's fingers danced in the air, energy crackling at the tips to form a spell. The warrior jumped into the fray and cut off Annabelle from her attackers. The spell crackled and fizzled at the interruption.

"Stone bearer," the emaciated witch seethed.

"Always nice to be recognized." Soriya smirked. The Greystone was already in hand. She felt it come to life as her will surged into the stone.

Wind swirled. The gale lifted from the ground and rushed through the street. Mercy's sisters flew back from the force, unable to stay aloft in the sudden assault. Mary slammed into a nearby car. She bounced off the hood and into the bumper of the vehicle in front of it. Maggie crashed through the window of a vacant home, the FOR RENT sign following her into the living room. Mercy landed on the ground. She planted her feet and leaned into the gale rather than let it overwhelm her.

"Enough," Mercy said. She raised her hand to flick Soriya aside.

The stone bearer had learned her lesson from their previous encounter. The ribbon of Kali snapped forward and wrapped tightly around Mercy's extended hand. The witch screamed, burning at the touch of death itself.

'Bring us pain?' Maggie shouted. Soriya fell to one knee from the force of Maggie's mental cry, and the ribbon went slack. Maggie crawled from the shattered glass of the home. *'Curse us. Ruin our good work.'*

Soriya shook her head. She covered her ears, then whipped the ribbon hard to the left, where Maggie was positioned. "I've had enough crazy for one night."

The ribbon snapped against Maggie's chest. The force slammed her through the window and back into the home.

The thin strands struggled to return; their abilities were held at bay by Mercy's renewed efforts.

"Then by all means," Mercy said through gritted teeth. She strained to keep the ribbon locked down. It continued to reel back toward Soriya. "Leave us to our work."

Mary was up and waiting. She struck out, energy dancing from her hands. Bolts of light shot from her fingertips toward the still kneeling Annabelle. Soriya's eyes widened in fear, and she forgot about the ribbon. She dove forward and knocked the scarlet-haired witch aside.

The bolts sent Soriya flying. She slammed into the side of an SUV, and the alarm activated from the impact. The ribbon returned to her, freed from Mercy's tampering, and slid up Soriya's arm. It acted as a protective salve to remove the pain from her collision.

Soriya stood in time to see the second set of blasts head for her. She dove to the right a split second ahead of the blast. The SUV took the impact. The driver's-side door caved in as the force sent the entire vehicle sliding onto the sidewalk and into the nearest home.

Maggie and Mercy joined the assault. Soriya kept moving. She never paused, never stopped, not for even a second. The moment her feet hit the ground, she was leaping again to avoid the next in the series. Blast after blast of concentrated spellwork pulled in ambient light from nearby and focused it into concussive force. She had never seen such spells before—not in all her training, not with such ease, and not to the sound of cackling laughter from her attackers.

Three on one were bad odds, even for Soriya, and the trio were too practiced at their craft. For every inch she gained, they sent her back a foot. Annabelle was caught in the middle of the fight, unable to find cover.

"Annabelle!" Soriya shouted as she narrowly survived another bolt—this time from the reinvigorated Maggie. "You have to stand up! You have to run!"

"Don't, Sister," Mercy replied. "That isn't what you really want."

"You're one of us, Sister," Mary said.

'She belongs with us,' Maggie screamed. Her mental cry caused Soriya to falter only a step, but it was enough to bring her crashing to the ground. *'Leave her to us.'*

"Can't," Soriya said. She rolled ahead, farther away from her goal, but out of reach of their power for the moment. Soriya jumped to her feet, stone in hand. "You're trying to hurt my friend there."

"Not your friend," Mary said. "Our family."

"You have no idea who she really is," Mercy said. "Or what she can do."

Annabelle perked up at Mercy's proclamation. "So tell me!"

'We will,' Maggie's thoughts bellowed through a staple-filled grin. *'We will show you everything.'*

"Run, Annabelle!"

But it was too late. All three sisters moved for their intended target. Soriya was too far away to intervene this time. Light encapsulated Annabelle, not from concussive force, but a sphere of energy that contained her.

Annabelle rushed to the side. Her body was immediately blasted back from the protection in the spellwork.

"Let her go!"

"We will," Mercy said. "When the time is right."

"Then spell it out for me," Soriya said. She took a step closer. Slow movements closed the gap between her and the Daughters. "Tell me who she is to you and why she's so important. I hate when people keep secrets from me."

Mercy raised her hand, and Soriya stopped, unable to press forward another inch. "You're out of your depth, Greystone. A child with all that power in your hands, yet you hold this city back. You keep it locked in place, unable to face the darkness within or prepare for the light to come."

"This was *our* great city," Mary declared as she showcased the city surrounding them. "From the very beginning it was ours."

'Time to finish this,' Maggie said. With one hand maintaining the link to the makeshift prison trapping Annabelle, the Daughters raised their free hands and took aim at Soriya. She tried to break free of Mercy's hold, but every effort came up short.

Concentrated light billowed from them. It shot forward, coalescing into a single stream. The blast battered Soriya back. She bounded off the roof of a Corolla and slammed into the vinyl-sided edifice of a home on the other side.

When Soriya tried to stand, she was met with the same light. It pinned her to the wall.

"I... I won't let you take her!"

"You have no choice," Mercy said. "We tried to do the right thing in our previous lives. We played by society's rules. We built this city from nothing, but were betrayed by the man who claimed the deed for himself."

'Red eyes.' Maggie's words hurt worse than the light locking Soriya in place. *'Traitor to us. The evil one.'*

Mary nodded in agreement. "*He* was supposed to be the chosen one. The one to show Portents the truth."

'Lies,' Maggie replied. *'Always lies.'*

"This time, we take matters in our own hands," Mercy said. "And our dear sister will see the light. One way or another."

"No," Soriya exclaimed. Her arms refused to cooperate. She couldn't even feel her legs anymore. Still, she fought against their efforts. Every ounce of her willpower poured through her. Soriya needed to keep Annabelle safe like she'd promised. "I won't—"

The wall crumbled behind her. The siding was torn off of the edifice, and the structure beneath broke from the force. The blast sent her through the wall and into the home. Her head collided with plaster before she hit the couch and crashed to the ground.

Cuts decorated her skin. Her arm hurt to lift, and her legs struggled to carry her weight. Standing caused black spots to dot her field of vision. She shuffled across the room to the hole in the wall.

The Daughters of Salem were already at the end of the block. They floated along without a care in the world. Behind them, carted along like a dog on a leash, was Annabelle. Her terror-filled eyes pleaded with the battered and broken Soriya.

The stone bearer tried to pursue. She made it two steps from the home before her legs gave way. Soriya fell to the sidewalk, hands barely able to keep her from slamming face-first to the ground. By the time she looked up again, the street was empty.

Annabelle was gone.

CHAPTER TWENTY-SIX

The gate fell with a crash. It shattered, leaving the hinges all but swinging in the breeze with nothing left to support. The metal had taken a beating for the last hour. The two beasts outside had been relentless in their assault, single-minded in their resolve to slaughter the two people inside.

Eddie tucked close to the wall of his shop and held the hammer before him. Slow breaths kept him from hyperventilating. Hanging clocks hid him from view, but they did nothing to stop the growling sounds from causing him to cower further against the tiny inlet.

"Why am I doing this again?" he whispered. Sweat coated his palms. He tried to wipe them clean along his pants—one at a time so he could maintain his death grip on the hammer. Nothing helped, and the sweat returned.

He couldn't believe his actions. He was risking his life, putting everything he had spent months building, for the sake of a complete stranger. A woman whose name he hadn't even learned.

"What am I, crazy?" he continued. "All this for a girl? Okay, so she's good-looking. And yeah, she smiled at you and held your hand while you were a blubbering fool. Is that enough to make me be an idiot and risk my life?"

Eddie crept from his position. He leaned closer to the corner of his small alcove for a glance outside. The twin beasts clambered over the security gate for the front door to the shop. He jumped back and accidentally slammed his head against the wall. Rubbing away his stupidity, Eddie let out a long, calming breath.

"Looks like it will have to be."

The glass shattered into the shop. The door snapped open, rattling back and forth against the frame, to give entry to one of the beasts. The other pounced on the window ledge and kicked away the remnants of glass before bounding inside. They howled in triumph.

Eddie pressed against the wall. He wished it would envelop him. More than that, though, he wished for another way out. The woman needed him, however. She was depending on him. She had put her life in his hands.

"This is stupid, Eddie," he breathed. "Really fucking stupid."

His words were barely audible to him. They were lost behind the beating of his heart pounding in his ears. Unfortunately, they had been loud enough to draw the attention of both of the monsters rummaging through the store.

The moment they shifted in his direction, Eddie had no choice. He screamed, and all the pent-up anger, frustration, and pure panic poured out of him. The hammer rose over his head as he raced from his hiding place and charged at the creatures.

He pummeled the closest with the hammer, driving the top of it down onto the back of the beast. The creature whimpered from the blow, then crashed to the ground.

Before Eddie could lift the hammer once more, the second slammed into him. Eddie fell to the ground with a thud. The claws of the beast ripped at his hands. The hammer nearly tumbled to the ground, but he kept a tight grip on it. Jaws snapped. The beast was atop him, drool running from his thick fangs. The day trader was gone. There was nothing left of the Italian-loafer-wearing money-man. Bloodshot eyes welled with tears, unwilling to even blink. They demanded Eddie's death, and it took every ounce of strength to keep the beast at bay.

Blood soaked Eddie's hands. The claws dug into his flesh. They felt like red-hot pokers being driven through him. Eddie screamed, yet kept the hammer raised.

"Oh no you don't," Eddie said through gritted teeth. He tucked his knees against his torso. "I am not getting eaten today. I have too much work to do."

He shot his feet out and connected solidly with the creature's gut. The monster rebounded immediately, but Eddie had already rolled away to the right. He shot up to his feet. Agony rose up his arms from his open wounds. He did his best to forget about the sixteen-hour shift he had put in before the madness started, and about the insane pressure of having someone's life on the line. Instead, he focused on the woman's drop-dead gorgeous eyes for inspiration.

When the beast landed on the spot Eddie had been, the shop owner swung the hammer. It slammed into the creature's cheek, knocking his head sharply to the right. The manic monster collapsed to the ground with a thud.

Eddie tried to catch his breath, but the first one growled for his attention. The beast rubbed at his sore back, unable to scratch the itch left by Eddie's initial blow. The creature seethed, snarling at the shopkeeper.

"Didn't you hear me the first time?" Eddie asked, hammer raised. "I said, no!"

Eddie clocked the beast hard on the side of the head. The creature's feet left the ground, and the mutated figure soared to the wall and crashed through the shelving units. He groaned as he fell to the floor, unconsciousness taking hold at last.

With his chest heaving and the hammer too heavy to continue to carry, Eddie slumped forward. The weapon slammed to the carpet, and the hilt followed suit quickly after. Eddie tried to slow his pounding heart.

"What the hell is wrong with you two?" Eddie asked when he found his nerve. He glanced around the shop. The shelves were shattered, his hard work all but ruined from the fight. "Look at the damn mess you made!"

The two beasts remained collapsed on the ground. A chuckle slipped from Eddie's lips at the absurdity of his words.

I did it, Eddie thought as he fell to his knees. His hand wiped away the layer of sweat on his brow. "Well, I'll be damned."

CHAPTER TWENTY-SEVEN

There were too many. The beasts no longer ransacked the businesses of the red-light district. Instead, they circled around an exhausted Mentor, waiting to end him.

A silver lining existed in the moment, as far as Mentor was concerned. The civilians had been cleared from the area. Most had managed to avoid discovery in their escape. Mentor had taken care of the rest. When the battle had begun and he had leapt into the fray with everything at his disposal, he had drawn the monsters toward him. Blow for blow, Mentor met the creatures head on. He battered them back, ducking and diving out of reach of their counterstrikes. He couldn't falter. He couldn't fail—not tonight of all nights.

It was his last night as the Greystone.

It was a silly distinction. Mentor knew he would never *truly* relinquish the role, but he was also aware that his time had become limited. The days ahead were greatly outnumbered by the days behind him. Soriya was the future, and he was merely passing the torch for the next generation.

His age and exhaustion, however, would not stand in his way against the beasts. There would be no quarter given, no respite offered to the transformed humans threatening Portents. Mentor dug in and drove them back. When he pressed forward, the stone was in his hand to light his way.

The rune sprung to life, and his will caused a glow to spread from the surface. The beasts retreated at the sight, though the moment was fleeting. Darkness quickly returned, and with it so did the tide of monsters. His efforts wavered. His will was not up to the task of tackling the threat.

The snarl of a creature woke Mentor to the true danger of his situation. The beast had snuck up close behind him and swiped at his back. A single claw caught his cloak, pulling at the tan fabric as Mentor dove to avoid the blow.

He hadn't even seen the beast. He had been too wiped from utilizing the Greystone. The creatures were too close for him to push back. It left him little choice but to run for cover. He needed space to regroup. It was only a matter of time before he was overrun.

If he fell, innocents would once again be put at risk. Mentor couldn't let that happen. Mentor jumped to avoid the swinging claws of the beasts blocking his escape. He somersaulted over the shoulder of one and landed at the creature's backside. The road was open in front of him.

His strategy was sound. The beasts, furious over his escape, followed with everything they had. Every ounce of rage was directed at him, exactly as he'd hoped. The only thing Mentor hadn't counted on were civilians running back to the fight.

Grace and Wes, the pair he had passed off to an officer of the law, dashed in his direction. The strong-willed and stubborn woman led her terrified friend toward Mentor.

"Run!" Mentor bellowed as he tried to wave them away. The pair skidded to a halt at the sight of the creatures chasing Mentor. The beasts were getting closer, and their howls filled the air. Mentor grabbed Grace, shaking her arm with frustration. "What the hell are you doing here?"

"It was her idea," Wes quickly commented, which drew a glare from Grace.

"We came back to see if you were—"

Mentor pushed her out of the way. The first of the creatures had already closed the distance. He swung his fist hard. It connected with the monster's chin and knocked the mutated human away. Then he turned back to the pair and pointed to the emptiness ahead.

"Move it!"

"Moving," Wes said. "We're moving!"

All three ran. Mentor prodded Grace ahead of him to avoid the fast-approaching beasts at their back. "I asked you to run," he said through heavy breaths. "You were supposed to get to safety."

Grace shrugged. "I'm a terrible listener."

"So it would seem," Mentor replied. He turned to Wes. "And you?"

"She made me do it."

"Wes!"

"What?" Wes said. "It's true."

"I hate you." Grace shook her head. "Now which way?"

Mentor hesitated. He wasn't sure how to answer. There was the potential to run into more innocents no matter what direction they chose. His brief delay caused Grace to take the lead. They made it to the next intersection—Pullman—then shot south. Halfway down the block, Grace cut left down an alley and into a dead end.

"Okay," Grace said, as she shuffled to the back wall. "I'm a worse navigator, it seems."

"What the hell, Grace?" Wes immediately started.

"I thought it cut through to Baker," Grace snapped. "Like you knew where to go."

"I know we have to get out of here before—"

The way was blocked. The beasts had covered the distance and now barred their escape. Four deep, they slowly entered the alley. Drool ran from their lips. The hunt was over.

Wes backed up to the wall. "Thanks a lot, Grace."

"Shut it, Wes," she said, then slapped his arm.

"You tried," Mentor said. "Just stay behind me."

Mentor puffed his chest. He stood before them, a barrier between them and the beasts. The Greystone sat tight against his right hand, and the pulsing warmth from its surface rushed up his arm.

"I'm not finished yet," he declared, stone at the ready. He held it before him. The beasts didn't flinch; they had no fear of his assault. There were too many to beat back, especially given the tight quarters. But if this was to be the end, Mentor would gladly give them a fight they would not forget.

"Good," a voice called from the street.

The beasts in front took a step forward. Mentor, however, peered past them at the back of the crowd. Creatures yelped, tossed from the rank and file by a pair of green-skinned hands. Others shifted toward the new threat, and a path opened in the center to reveal the seven-foot orc knocking them aside as he cut through the horde to join Mentor.

"Urg?"

"Holy crap!" Wes exclaimed, his voice cracking. He cowered close to Grace. "Another one! And it talks!"

Urg rolled his eyes. "Really, guy? Take your lady and get out of here already."

He turned and punched the closest beast in the face. Then Urg grabbed the transformed man and tossed him into the pack at the mouth of the alley. The beasts scattered for the open street.

"*Now* would be good," Urg said.

Wes was quick to move. Grace, however, stopped beside Mentor. Her hand fell on his arm, a saddened gaze locked on his.

"Do as he says," Mentor said. He cocked his head for the road. "Go take care of your friend."

"I will," Grace said. "Thank you."

Urg led the way to the street. He used his body as a shield, blocking the rampaging beasts to give Grace and Wes a clear path. Claws ripped at his skin and swiped the air around him, but Urg beat them back to allow the pair time for their escape. Grace and Wes retreated into the shadows, leaving Mentor and Urg to the monsters regrouping in the middle of the street.

"What happened to your suit?" Mentor asked. He took his

position at Urg's back to cover the right flank with fists raised and renewed hope.

Urg groaned. "I don't want to talk about it."

"How are things looking?"

"I've seen worse, but not by much," Urg said. He cracked his knuckles as he scanned the block. The beasts howled at their foes. Dozens gathered on both sides. "You up for this?"

Mentor smirked. He raised the stone and felt the light grow along the surface. "Let's get to work."

CHAPTER TWENTY-EIGHT

Annabelle tried to escape, but every effort was blocked. Her spells, frantic and ill-prepared, were repelled in turn. Nothing she attempted made a dent into the sphere that pulled her through the city and toward the western border.

The spires of downtown shifted through the apartment complexes and residential neighborhoods of Junction Cove to the grassy shores of Rose Riley Forest. The tree line took over, the forest overshadowing them along the mountainous hillside.

As the group passed through the thickening brush, Annabelle's attempts at escape faded. She was lost in the wilds of the forest and could only listen to the sound of the wind through the leaves and the wildlife surrounding them.

Once inside the confines of the forest, the group began their climb. The incline was steep, though the thin paths in the dirt made for a slow journey. The city opened up below, spread forth like a grand canvas against the night sky. From her vantage, she could see the small blazes of the red-light district mixed with the shadow of Evans Tower, and the glistening water of the port against the horizon. All came together to paint Portents as a thing of beauty—a living, breathing entity made whole through the sum of her parts.

It was magnificent to behold.

Yet it was nothing compared to the forest itself. The trio of witches continued their climb ever deeper into the foliage, only to come upon a wide clearing. Trees made up the outskirts in a circle to encapsulate the space. In the center was an altar carved from the stump of a tree. The thickness was a testimony to the tree's age before it had been cut down and repurposed as an altar.

Rising from the earth in a semi-circle around the altar were seven stone monoliths. All were sharpened at their peaks like great spears shooting from the ground. Carved into their faces were runes. They matched the tattoos adorning Annabelle's skin.

"What…" Annabelle started. Wary of receiving another shock, she pulled from the sides. Annabelle stood and faced her captors from the center of the sphere. "What is this place?"

Maggie's mental cry filled Annabelle's head with excitement. *'Home.'*

Mary's free hand waved across the landscape. It seemed to be how she sensed the environment, due to her lack of sight. "It's still here. Undisturbed."

"Good."

The sphere fell away, and Annabelle dropped to the ground. Leaves flew at her sudden arrival. Her fingers kneaded the earth as she lifted herself from the pile. She felt the power of the place. It was in the earth, carried through the spears and up toward the sky. There was a constant flow of energy that pulsed with each breath.

"No one comes here," Annabelle said. She took a seat upon the leaves. "They say it isn't safe."

"We made it that way," Mary replied with a satisfied smile. "The essence of fear is a powerful tool."

"You should know that, Sister," Mercy said.

All three ended their hovering. They joined her on the ground, bare feet kicking at the layers of leaves covering the grass. They circled Annabelle, hands at the ready.

"Stop calling me that," Annabelle snapped in disgust. "I'm nothing like you."

'Foolish lost child,' Maggie shouted through her head.

Mary turned to her older sibling. "How can she still not sense it? How can she still not see the truth?"

"What truth?" Annabelle said. "You're hideous monsters."

The Daughters shared a chuckle over her comment. Their laughter filled the silence of the forest. Annabelle tucked her knees close, unable to look at them any longer.

Mercy shifted by her side. "Once, we looked just like you."

Her hand shimmered before Annabelle. Light danced from the tips of her fingers to create a vision of days long since past. The night of the forest changed to the brightest of days.

As the sun shone down on them, three women laughed and played among the trees. Each had scarlet locks and flawless skin. Emerald eyes shimmered under the daylight. The women ran around the woods as if they owned them, content to be together—to live and love as one.

"Once we *were* you," Mercy whispered in Annabelle's ear.

Maggie's words echoed her sister's response. *'Beautiful and free.'*

Mary moved to the other side of Annabelle. "We lost everything to a mistake."

The images turned from joy to terror. The sun faded, and the laughter shifted to screams. The three sisters had wanted nothing than to bring joy to the world, yet now fought for survival. Red eyes beamed from the woods. The twin irises of crimson made the trees look like they were bleeding.

"We went too far," Mercy said. "We called upon forces more powerful than we had prepared for. Control was lost. When we sought out help and tried to make things right, we were betrayed."

Annabelle watched the scene unfold as Mercy told it. A man sat upon his throne at the heart of the city. His followers swarmed the sisters, tearing them apart with their brutality all while the man looked on with wide, red eyes of pleasure at the act. They burned before Annabelle. The flames ripped them from the world and stole every ounce of good they'd put into the city of Portents.

"You can change that," Mary said. "Our return was incomplete. You can bring us back completely and make us whole."

The images faded. Mercy snapped her fingers, and the woods returned. Then the eldest of the Daughters swiped at her sister, driving her away from Annabelle.

"Fool," she said in anger. "That does not matter compared to our task. The voice calls to us to finish what we started. It needs release."

"The voice?" Annabelle asked. She covered her ears in an attempt to blot out the screams of the sisters as they burned to death. She tried to push away the feeling of betrayal left by the people they had brought together at the founding of Portents. The sisters had provided protection for all of them in the early days. She saw everything thanks to Mercy's magic.

"You hear it, too," Mercy said with a nod. "It is why you opened the door. You didn't realize its influence, but it is always there. Pushing us. Defining us."

Could it be possible? Everything Mercy said resonated within Annabelle's thoughts. Her words rationalized so much of what Annabelle had attempted when opening the doors. More than that, it explained the years of research and the study of magic in the first place. An outside influence had pressed her to the task, and she had accepted without question, believing the reasons to be her own. She had been unaware of the presence whispering in her ear. How else would she have thought of the door in the first place? Why would she have even had the notion?

Annabelle stood, then wiped her hands clean along her cloak. "What is it? Where does the voice come from?"

"Your true home," Mercy explained.

'It is family,' Maggie said. *'It is pure light. It is everything.'*

"That…" Annabelle stopped. Every door she had opened came at a price. It had never brought her answers or family or even an ounce of light. "No. Whatever it is only ever brings monsters and darkness."

Mercy shook her head. "You lack control. Much as we did. We can help, Sister."

"Why?" Annabelle asked as she backed away from them. She stumbled at the edge of the altar, stumbling along the tree trunk. "Why do you keep calling me that?"

"Waterhouse," Mercy said. Annabelle's mouth fell open. She had never mentioned her last name, yet they knew it somehow. "Your name. It marked you as one of us."

"What?"

"A Daughter of Salem," Mary said. "Your ancestor was one of us."

"No," Annabelle muttered. "That's not possible."

"You feel it," Mercy pressed. "You know it is the truth. We are your family. We can show you the truth behind everything."

"A new world," Mary said.

Mercy held out her hand. "Open one last door, Annabelle."

"Bring the light out." Mary took her sister's hand.

Maggie reached for them, and her voice echoed along the altar. *'Change everything.'*

The evidence was there. She could see it, even through their monstrous forms. Everything fell into place and lined up with their story. Annabelle could see herself in them, in their experiences and their tragedies.

All three stood before her. They waited for her hand to join theirs—the Daughters of Salem at last fully reunited.

"Open the door, and we promise you all the answers you've sought," Mercy said. "Only we can give you that."

CHAPTER TWENTY-NINE

Soriya was still cursing herself when she returned to the Ver-trum home. The door banged against the frame from the driving wind rushing down the street. It struggled to open, forcing her to slam it out of her path.

Pain shot up her arm. She had been tossed aside, wrenched by the single flick of a damn finger, and sent crashing through windows and homes like a puppet. Her body had grown tired of the abuse. The toll she paid was due to her own arrogance. She'd believed Annabelle to be safe inside the home while she went out to protect Portents.

Instead, she had played into the Daughters' hands. They had instigated the violence, but the men and women who had been affected were merely a symptom of a much larger issue. Now that the sisters had Annabelle in their grasp, there was no telling what damage they might cause. Soriya had retreated to the his-torical landmark to regroup.

Soriya couldn't let anything more happen to Portents. That was her eternal edict, but it meant more to her tonight of all nights. This was supposed to be the night of her final test, a simple game to prove her worth as the Greystone. It had be-come a danger that threatened her home.

Soriya shook away her self-loathing and the doubts that had plagued her so much in the past. It wasn't the time for any of her fears to take hold. There were more important matters at hand. With renewed purpose, Soriya moved deeper into the darkness of the home. She took the steps to the lower level and the treasure trove hidden from the public.

The Vertrum home was more than a place for Soriya to lick her wounds. She required the knowledge contained in the place. Soriya had barely scratched the surface when it came to the Daughters of Salem. That lack of intel on their mysterious pasts was a detriment she could no longer ignore.

The Daughters had been a presence in Portents from the beginning. There wasn't a single account of their activities after the witch trials in Salem, not until their arrival in the city. No, for all intents and purposes they had done nothing at all with their lives... until Portents.

Something had drawn them to Soriya's city. They had joined the ranks of William Rath and the other founders in bringing settlers to Portents. They had stayed, but why?

Soriya returned to the texts that had drawn her to the home in the first place. She flipped through first-person accounts—those of Alexander Vertrum and more—all with the hope of learning everything she could about the trio of witches. None were specific as to the Daughters' plans.

The only clue came from a painting. The image was of the sisters in front of a cottage. Where most people occupied spaces at the heart of the fledgling city, the Daughters had separated themselves from the masses. They took up residence outside Portents' ever-widening borders. Nature appeared to have been their sanctuary, and their home was surrounded by woods.

Soriya flipped fervently through the paintings kept in the basement of the Vertrum home. With each, she learned more about the location. There was one of a cottage in the woods. Another depicted the three women standing near a series of stone outcroppings: monoliths decorated with runic sigils.

She sensed the power of the space, even through a single image painted over a century earlier. None of that mattered at the moment. The only thing of interest was the view from the hidden place. It overlooked the city, the tree line fading as the newly founded Portents stretched out to the horizon.

There was only one place such a view existed. It was a perspective unique to one location in Portents: Rose Riley Forest, or the Forest of the Veil as it was originally known.

The lead was all Soriya had to go on. She hoped it would be

enough. Soriya placed the images back against the corner of the secret space. She raced for the stairs and locked the hidden treasures up before she took to the streets once more. Soriya had to move quickly. She could feel the change in the air. Whatever the Daughters were planning was coming.

Time was running out.

CHAPTER THIRTY

Mercy and the Daughters held firm, waiting for the answer from one of their own. The evidence had been presented to Annabelle. She had been shown the secrets of their past. They had done everything they could to build Portents up from nothing, yet their efforts had been met with derision and betrayal. The prejudice for their magic caused nothing but outright hatred from the populace. When they'd attempted to plead their case with the first Mayor of Portents, they learned the truth of their situation.

Nathaniel Evans had been the one to turn everyone against them. It was a name Mercy had sworn from then on to never say aloud. Even the history books appeared to have stripped the man's relevance from view. Still, his impact on their lives had become embedded in her memory and that of her sisters.

Every memory had been shared with Annabelle Waterhouse.

Annabelle's ancestor had been one of them: a Daughter of Salem. So why had she not been pulled back with the others? Mercy had a theory, though it was one she did not bother to share. None of the others had children. The Waterhouse line had continued through the centuries up until the present. Annabelle's ancestor remained on the other side because of that. Her descendant had taken her place of power in the world.

So much power...

Mercy needed it. Portents did as well, but that would always be secondary. Mary had been right in that regard. Every glance at her emaciated form made her want to retch. They needed to be brought back whole. They needed to be beautiful once more.

Annabelle continued to mull over her options. Mercy attempted to hide her disdain. There were no true options for the girl, though her ignorance clouded her every judgment. Minutes of silence ended when she turned to their gathering.

"No," she said. "I won't do it."

"No?" Mercy shot a brief look toward her sisters. Clasped hands fell away from each other; Annabelle's decision shattered the solidarity of their sisterhood. Mary and Maggie rounded the exposed semi-circle in front of the seven stone monoliths and the altar Annabelle sat atop.

"You've hurt people," Annabelle continued. "That's all you've done since you came back. I want answers to my power and to my past. But not at the expense of others."

All the weight of her decision fell from her shoulders, and the great burden finally released. Mercy could see it in her eyes. There was pain in them from never truly knowing her place. It had driven the young woman to seek out answers through magic and the doorways to other realms. Annabelle sought out power, yet she had only found the Daughters waiting for her at the end of her journey.

The thought caused Mercy to laugh, and the sound echoed through the trees. Mary and Maggie joined in the fun. The laughter took them back to better days of freedom, where the world bowed before them or paid the price.

Those days would come again.

Annabelle stood, looming over them from atop the altar. "Did I say something funny?"

Mercy sighed, then wiped at the tear resting in the corner of her eye. She flicked it to the ground. "Honestly? We cared little for your decision."

Annabelle's defiance wilted to fear. She clearly realized her stubbornness didn't matter in the end. She frantically searched for some means of escape, but the sisters surrounded her. Annabelle's eyes widened when she noticed she was standing in the center of the altar—right where the Daughters wanted her.

"I won't open the door for you!" Annabelle shouted. "You'll never get anything from me."

"We already have."

Annabelle rushed for the grass, but the effort came too late. Mercy and the others raised their hands—the chant was already on their lips.

"Induma forlocto ceridia nachte."

The words came from a dead language. They had been written in caves and in the deepest recesses of pits long since forgotten. Each held power and brought light to the forest.

A binding sphere enveloped Annabelle. She slammed against the side and back to the center of the altar with a thud. Her pain was only beginning.

Mercy increased the volume and energy of her chanting. The light continued to spread, widening to engulf the altar completely. It reached the edge of the stone monoliths. Each in turn came to life, and the runes etched upon them glowed in response.

Annabelle screamed. She kicked and punched at the barrier. Each strike was repelled, however, and the shock eventually forced her to her knees.

Maggie tilted her head, the staples upon her lips glinting in the light. *'Trapped. Stuck.'*

"What is this?" Annabelle asked. There was fear in her voice.

"We tried to show you the darkness," Mercy said. She pointed toward the city in the distance. "Those beasts on the street? They aren't aberrations. That is what is inside all of them—all of humanity. They bring nothing but darkness to the world."

"All we will bring them is the light," Mary continued.

"How?"

"By giving you your truth," Mercy replied. "That's what you've been asking for, isn't it?"

Mary smiled. "Consider it a final gift from your family."

All three shifted closer to the sphere. The light grew. Annabelle pulled at the sleeves of her flowing green cloak. The runes on her skin, the birthright passed down from her ancestor, began to burn bright with power. They started at her wrists and moved upward. Annabelle's cries intensified as her arms were overtaken by the Daughters' spell.

"Let the ceremony begin."

CHAPTER THIRTY-ONE

Eddie hovered over the defeated creatures at his feet. He refused to look away in case they woke up. His heart continued to pound, and he once again picked up the hammer. It was a preventative measure, but the way he was feeling, he would have offered little in the way of resistance if the fighting started up again.

Shuffling steps and the creaking of floorboards rose up behind him. Eddie gripped the hammer tighter. He spun around, yelling as he swung the weapon in front of him to block the newcomer to the room.

The woman he had been trying to protect flinched and jumped back. Her hands waved in front of her. A cry slipped from her lips, surprise and panic rolled into one.

Eddie recognized the feeling very well.

"Sorry," he muttered, dropping the hammer. It clattered at his feet. "I'm sorry. I wasn't sure—"

She ran up to him and wrapped her arms tight to his sides in a hug. "You're okay."

The aches from a moment earlier were gone. Eddie's hands grasped her back and held her tight. It lasted only a second, but went on forever in his mind. Her warmth and spirit resuscitated him, and he remembered what the insanity had all been for.

A stray glance caught the beasts at their feet. Eddie's concern grew with each subtle shift of their sleeping bodies. He pulled away from the woman and took her by the hand. "What are you doing out here? You should be—"

"I heard the fight and then..." She stopped. Her eyes

washed over the scene and then over him, stopping at the deep scratches and blood on his hands. "And then there was nothing. I was scared for you."

"Come on," Eddie said. He moved for the back room, then decided against it. Trapping themselves would do nothing to keep the woman safe. They needed to head somewhere else, somewhere better than his hole-in-the-wall shop surrounded by memories of their long night. "We should get you somewhere safe before—"

"I have to go."

"Oh." He had forgotten. She'd told him about the bar where she worked. Her friends had been there, and she had run out on everyone to save herself. Her concern was likely focused on the people that mattered to her.

Before she could reach the door, Eddie cut her off. "Listen," he said, trying to hide his disappointment. "I don't think it's safe to go back there yet. I don't—"

"It's my mom," the woman said. She tucked her hair back, the purple highlights beaming under the lamp light from outside. "She's not far from here. I can't... I need to know she's all right with everything that's happened. I..."

"I get it."

He stepped out of the way to give her room. She nodded, a look of appreciation on her face. She reached for the door, but the knob broke loose the moment she touched it. Turning back to him with a sheepish look, she passed him the useless handle. Rather than mess with the door, the woman stepped through the shattered glass at the center for the sidewalk outside.

"It's not far," she replied. "I'll be okay. Thanks to you."

"Are you sure?" Eddie called after her. He followed her to the sidewalk. Rather than continue toward the marketplace, she shifted close to him.

"I'll be safe. Thank you." Standing on the tips of her toes, she kissed him. Surprise quickly settled to pleasure, and he embraced her. He felt like he was floating. Both smiled when it ended. "As a rule, I don't usually kiss guys when I don't know their name."

Eddie laughed. "Good to know."

She kissed him again; her soft lips melted over his. How much time passed, he couldn't say, but he hoped it would never end. Eventually, she settled on her heels, and her fingertip grazed her lips.

Eddie almost fell forward. He blinked hard to regain what little composure he had. "It's... it's Eddie. My name."

"Sherry," she said. Her hand ran along his cheek. "Thank you, Eddie."

"Thank... Thank you, too."

Sherry headed off into the night. At the corner she turned north toward the residential neighborhoods outside Allure, away from the red-light district. Eddie stood in the center of the sidewalk, unable to think or speak for a long time. He merely watched her depart and wondered if he would ever see her again.

Once he no longer heard her steps in the distance, Eddie sighed. He slapped his forehead and kicked at the ground. "Thank you, too?" he groaned. "What the hell is wrong with me?" Eddie pulled at his hair as he shuffled back to the shop. "No, I can't escort you home. Why? Because I'm a friggin idiot, that's why. Absolutely clueless, Eddie, that's what you are."

Glass crunched beneath his feet. Debris scattered around the shop. Displays were ruined, and weeks-long projects had been destroyed. The devastation added to the mounting aggravation. Eddie's shoulders slumped at the clean-up to come.

"You couldn't just walk her home, could you, Eddie?" he said in the silence of the shop. "No, you'd much rather wait for these monsters to wake up and finish the job they've started on my store. Idiot!"

The two creatures shifted and stirred, their sleep interrupted by his shouting. Eddie immediately covered his mouth and crossed the store. The hammer was on the opposite end.

"Speaking of waking up..." Eddie whispered. His eyes never left the slowly shifting bodies beneath him. He stopped short of the hammer, distracted by the low hue of light emanating from his sleeping enemies. "What the hell?"

The radiance billowed from the beasts. It shimmered along their skin, then flowed in a steady stream. The light rose free from the unconscious figures on the ground and floated next to the befuddled Eddie. It filled the room with an eerie glow.

The two small streams coalesced in a path for the door and the outside world. The concentrated light soared from the shop, leaving Eddie once again in darkness.

The beasts were gone. When the light departed, apparently the curse had left as well. Two men remained, though their clothes were still in tatters. Their claws and fangs were gone, but the bruises from their battle remained.

Eddie followed the trail of light to the street, watching as it shifted west for the outskirts of town, where dozens of other streams floated like a wave toward the west of the city. Confused, bruised, and battered, Eddie rubbed at his neck, wondering what the hell could possibly happen next. "Definitely not the kind of night I was expecting. Not at all."

CHAPTER THIRTY-TWO

Mentor and Urg remained back-to-back, prepared for the fight of their lives. All other civilians had cleared the district. It left the door open for the pair to finally strike without fear of collateral damage.

They drew the creatures in. The twisted versions of average people were cautious, but their need was clearly too great. They seemed to crave violence like a physical compulsion, as if their very existence depended on wholesale slaughter.

Once within range, Mentor offered the slightest of nods to the orc at his back. Urg read the motion with barely a glance. His fist shot out, crashing into the closest monster to drive it into the pack. Mentor pushed away from his companion and into the fight.

Urg's assault was brutal. Even though it was difficult to navigate against the horde's numbers, he used his strength to its full advantage. He pounded at the beasts in range, battering them aside like they were nothing more than ragdolls. His rock-hard skin kept any injuries sustained to a minimum. A beast's jaws clamped down on his bicep for a snack, and Urg simply lifted the creature from the ground while looking in frustration at the tatters of his shirt caught in the twisted man's teeth. He pulled the beast loose and tossed him into the crowd.

Mentor saw all that happen in a flash. His concern remained on each carefully placed blow to the men and women of his city who had somehow succumbed to an outside force.

There were too many to handle, and the hours of fighting had taken their toll on Mentor. He needed to thin the herd rushing at him.

The Greystone served him well. A wall of light sent the creatures soaring. They crashed through neighboring shop windows and slammed against parked cars. The stone was a crutch, however, and one with diminishing returns. Each attempt to utilize the ancient weapon drained him further.

The beasts were back on him in seconds. They drove Mentor closer to Urg. He delivered an uppercut on the first, a roundhouse kick into the second, but still they came.

"This is more than simple possession," Mentor said as he struggled to push his attackers back. "These people have been altered somehow."

"Magic," Urg replied. He swept his arm around. It crashed into the chest of a beast wearing overalls and pigtails. She slammed into three of her kin, sending them to the pavement in a heap. "This was magic."

"Powerful magic, then."

"I saw them," Urg said. "The ones who did this were grotesque women. Definitely not human any longer. They were chanting some kind of spell. I heard them when they dropped the mist on the ground. But I don't know what they were saying. The language was... old. That was the last thing I remember before I changed."

Witches. It was the only possible explanation. Yet, where had they come from? In all his studies, witchcraft had been a rarity. For all the power and all the secrets of the universe at his disposal, Mentor had never come against such a threat before. Magic was unnatural, and it pulled at darker forces than even the worst myth and legend that tended to terrorize the city.

"Who are they?"

"No idea," Urg answered. He grabbed the heads of two more creatures and smashed them against each other. They crumpled to the ground at his feet. "What do you think they're after with all this?"

"I wish I knew," Mentor said. He ducked beneath the swiping claw of a large man. The second the blow passed over him, Mentor drove up with his fist. It collided against the creature's chin. Mentor was at the next threat before the beast hit the ground.

"Think Soriya knows?"

"What?" Urg's question made Mentor pause. His guard dropped, and his fists unclenched as his ward's name filled his every thought. Distracted, he failed to notice two beasts moving in for the kill behind him. Urg lifted one of the crumpled creatures at his feet and threw it at the pair about to blindside Mentor. The beast crashed into them and they fell to the pavement.

Mentor shook his head to snap himself back to the present. "Thank you."

"Don't mention it," Urg said. He shifted close, blocking Mentor from the fight. "You don't know where she is, do you?"

"No." Her final test had been designed that way. Their game of hide-and-seek had been about them enjoying one last night of fun before the burden fell solely upon her shoulders. He had wanted her to remember the joy that could come from the task. He had surely picked the wrong night.

"No?"

"No," Mentor repeated as he rejoined the fight. "But I've learned enough about Soriya over the years to know she's always exactly where she's needed. Just as we are right now."

He held out the Greystone. Urg offered a nod, then dropped to the ground. The beasts did not see the attack coming until it was too late.

A wave of energy crashed into them. The beasts rocketed down the steet. They slammed through the broken windows of neighboring buildings. It was the most intense strike Mentor could envision, but he knew it had cost him.

When the light diminished, Mentor nearly collapsed. Urg caught him and kept him on his feet. Mentor gave a gracious smile.

Both looked around. The block was clear of conscious threats. The dozens still in sight lay on the ground or leaned against buildings, cars, and mailboxes.

"That all of them?" Urg asked. "I thought there were more."

"Are you complaining?" Mentor said. The dizziness from his strike began to wear off, and he tried to stand on his own. Urg reached to assist him, but Mentor waved him off. He only needed another second.

"Nope," Urg said. "No complaints at all. I am perfectly fine with that."

"Good."

Mentor's brow furrowed. Light began to ripple along the unconscious forms on the street. He shuffled to the closest one and watched the stream of light grow. It floated from the monster, then coalesced with the streams of a dozen more before heading off into the distance.

The beast was gone. In place of the malicious creature was a man. His body rested on the pavement. The same held true for the men and women strewn about the scene. The light receded, and with it the spell that had infected them all.

"What do you think that means?" Urg asked.

"I think those women you mentioned just moved on to the main event."

The light flowed into a single, concentrated form and headed west for the outskirts of the city. After a moment,the energy faded behind the tree line at the outskirts of Rose Riley Forest.

"You asked where Soriya is, Urg." Mentor pointed to the woods. "She's where she always is. Right at the center of the storm."

CHAPTER THIRTY-THREE

Soriya crept through the forest and stayed low to the ground, trying her best to keep quiet. She hid behind a wall of growing evergreens. Standing against three potent threats, Soriya needed every advantage available to her—starting with the element of surprise.

However, it was Soriya who ended up being surprised.

Beyond the tree line was a clearing. Seven stone monoliths were positioned in a semi-circle. They were exactly as they had been depicted in the image she'd found at the Vertrum home. Nothing had changed, despite the century between the painting and now. They did not appear weathered by age or the constant shift of seasons. The runic sigils upon them were bold and bright, made even more so by the arrival of the stream of energy floating from the city.

Annabelle stood between the monoliths. Trapped in a wall of protoplasmic energy, the same ball of light that had pulled her from Soriya earlier that night, she tried to fight for her freedom. Her attempts were met with pain. The shock battered her back to the center of the glowing sphere, which was made stronger by the arriving energy.

"*Futilinano, spacitati, minascala,*" the sisters chanted as one. The three sisters stood some distance from each other. It was unlike any language Soriya had ever heard. Their purpose made no sense—not until she saw the results take form in the clearing.

Bolts of light shifted from the sister's hands as their spell grew in strength. The bolts passed through the barrier of Annabelle's prison cell and slammed into their hostage, causing her to scream.

"Stop!" Annabelle cried. "Please stop!"

The glyphs on her arms sparked. Tiny flames decorated her flesh as the runic tattoos were activated by the spell. Light showered from her. It was forcibly pulled into the clearing, and a door began to take shape.

The chanting continued, more and more spirited, as the door came into view. It was flooded with Bypass energy. The conduit to other worlds was unlocked for the sisters thanks to Annabelle. The Daughters of Salem exploited her connection.

This wasn't about righting some betrayal from their former lives. Their need for the doormaker was about bringing something over with them. This was about another escape—another threat. Every death had been in service to another. It was why they had come back, and why they had possibly come to Portents in the first place.

Whatever terror hid on the other side of the door, Soriya couldn't allow it entrance. If it managed to find its footing in reality, there might be no way of stopping it.

"This has gone on long enough," Soriya muttered.

Standing from her cover behind the trees, Soriya removed the stone along her hip. The ribbon of Kali slid from her left arm and danced along the wind down her side.

Soriya leapt into the clearing between the Daughters. The ribbon snapped wide, then crashed against Mercy to the left and Mary to the right. The sudden assault broke their chanting and ended their connection to Annabelle and the doorway.

The portal to the Bypass started to close.

"No!" Mercy screamed.

The ribbon whipped back to Soriya's side. The stubborn protector offered a smirk at her ill-tempered foes. "Sorry, but this ends now."

CHAPTER THIRTY-FOUR

"You have to fight this, Annabelle!"

Soriya was a blur. With three attacking her at once, she had little choice. She had learned that the hard way at their previous encounter. Battered and bruised, Soriya ducked and dodged through the minefield created by the Daughters' magic. She was unwilling to surrender to the inevitable.

"Kill the Greystone!" Mercy bellowed.

The door remained in view. Even with their concentration divided, the door continued to form—albeit slowly. The cloaked woman locked on the altar cried out in pain. The light still billowed from the tattoos along her arms. Each rune beamed brightly like a spotlight in the sky.

Soriya needed her to fight through the pain. She needed the scarlet-haired Wiccan to stand with her. Time was against them as the Daughters regrouped from Soriya's surprise arrival.

'My pleasure!' Maggie yelled.

Soriya slid beneath a blast from Mary, skidding against the slick grass. Leaves flew into the air to create a natural barrier from the others. Once clear of the strike, Soriya kicked out and leapt at Maggie.

"You have it backward," Soriya said as she cocked back her fist. Unloading on the unprepared Maggie, Soriya's blow slammed into the woman's chin. Staples flew loose from her lips as the witch staggered. A kick to the gut sent her crashing into a tree on the outskirts of the clearing. Her head bashed against the bark and she collapsed against the ground, her mental anguish finally silenced.

"Get away from our sister!" Mercy screamed.

Mercy and Mary unleashed hell on Soriya. Blasts cut through the foliage, and the concussive force of their magical anger kicked up dirt and debris from all around Soriya. She tried to avoid what she could, jumping out of the line of fire just before it arrived. The aftershocks were another matter entirely. The earth cracked and shattered, and the sudden shifts of the ground knocked Soriya away from the stone monoliths.

Soriya picked herself up from the wet grass. Dirt was caked to her bloodied arms. "I need you to fight this, Annabelle."

"I... I can't!" Annabelle said. The light took over. The door took shape in the clearing, powered by the altar, the monoliths, and the witch's magic. All was funneled through Annabelle, whose control had never been tested to this level. The doors had opened to unknown realms and unexpected threats during her previous attempts. With the Daughters' guidance, who knew what could escape from beyond the veil of time and space.

"You have to!" Soriya shouted over Annabelle's cries. "Fight them, Annabelle. Stop them!"

The door flickered and fluctuated. The ethereal green glow swirled, and the form of the mystic frame in the clearing faded. Mary waved her hands before the door, panic stretched across the chasms where her eyes once were.

"Sister," she called to Mercy. "She resists us."

"I'm well aware, dear," Mercy said with a sneer. A stray blast rocked the tree behind Soriya. Its trunk cracked from the impact. The tree toppled forward, tumbling for the earth. Soriya raced to escape the growing shadow. She dove clear before the heavy oak crashed behind her.

"No," Mary replied. Her attention turned to the altar. "They *both* do."

Annabelle stood. Fighting through the pain, the young witch faced her captors. "I won't be used by you," she said through gritted teeth.

Mercy and Mary ignored the dazed Soriya. Mary's chanting resumed, and power pulsed from their fingers. The renewed force brought Annabelle low once more.

The door snapped into place, stronger than before.

"You have no choice, Sister!" Mercy yelled over the wails of her victim and the crackling force of the energy dominating the clearing. "You are the link. You opened the door for us. This is what you've always wanted. Don't resist. Let the light come."

"I… won't…" Annabelle's words were desperate. Soriya could barely see her through the light emanating from the runes on her skin. The door hovered just off the ground, a fully formed connection to the Bypass.

"You wanted the truth, dear," Mercy said. "You wanted to know your true home, the place you truly belonged. That was our promise to you. It's here! It's coming!"

Leaping over the trunk of a fallen tree, Soriya rushed for the door and the two still-standing sisters. A figure came out of no-where and knocked Soriya aside. She had forgotten about Maggie, but the manic witch had not forgotten her. They struggled along the ground, clawing and kicking at each other.

'Hate Greystone,' Maggie cried. 'Never stand with us. Always hurt us.'

"What can I say?" Soriya replied. She caught Maggie by the wrists and shoved her aside. Diving atop the witch, Soriya pummeled her with blow after blow. "I just *really* don't like you."

'Sisters!' Maggie yelled. Her mental cry shook the others from their mission. The energy fizzled from the altar.

Soriya smirked. She punched Maggie across the face, knocking her unconscious. Soriya turned to confront the other sisters. "Who's next?"

"It doesn't matter, Greystone," Mercy said. "Fight. Battle. Struggle against the rising tide. You will always fall short. We have already won."

The door was still there. Even with their attention diverted, the door remained in the clearing. From inside the swirling mass of green energy, shapes took form. Light and shadow formed worlds beyond and faces in the mist. Whatever danger they had called was getting closer by the second.

There was no more time.

"No," Soriya said. "You *thought* you won. There's a differ-ence."

She took off like a shot, no longer concerned with the fight in front of her. Soriya ran for all she was worth toward the sphere of energy and the woman trapped within. As she sprinted, Soriya removed the Greystone at her side and held it before her.

"What are you——?"

"Stop her!" Mercy shouted.

Mary's blast went wide.

Annabelle held her hands out, trying to block Soriya when she reached the threshold of the altar. "Soriya, don't!"

The Greystone cut a hole through the sphere, and Soriya burst through. The stone shared the same purpose as Annabelle's magic: to tap into the Bypass. The stone, though, worked to protect rather than exploit the energies trapped within the enigmatic object. Soriya landed next to Annabelle. She offered a smile, distracting the overwhelmed doormaker. Without hesitation or explanation, Soriya's hands shot out. She caught Annabelle in the chest and pushed her from the altar through the hole she had poked in the sphere. Annabelle fell to the ground with a thud.

"Soriya!" Annabelle tried to get back to the altar, but the hole had closed.

"No choice, Annabelle," Soriya said. She reached for the woman's hand, only to be repelled by the fierce electrical storm flowing from the stone monoliths. "Now run!"

CHAPTER THIRTY-FIVE

Annabelle was free. Her skin no longer felt like there were hot pokers digging into her. The light had faded from the runes tattooed upon her flesh. All that remained was the sweat on her skin and the wet grass of the forest beneath her.

She wanted to run. That was her first instinct—to get the hell out of the way and let the true protector of Portents do the job.

Soriya's scream kept Annabelle locked in place. Her feet refused to listen to reason. Her body was unable to comply with her terrified demands to run and never look back. She was still just as trapped as the woman who had saved her.

The spell continued to unfold. The door remained despite losing Annabelle as the critical component. Somehow, the circuit was intact. It continued to flow from the stone monoliths into the sphere, through Soriya, and out to the door.

Soriya had failed to disrupt the circuit; she had merely taken Annabelle's place. Soriya did not carry the same lineage that Annabelle had discovered during her captivity, nor the tattoos that allowed her access to other worlds. Without the protection offered by the tattoos, Soriya's agony appeared more intense than anything Annabelle had endured.

Annabelle was one of the Daughters. Soriya was something else entirely. The difference seemed to cause nothing but pain, and the warrior dropped to her knees. The energies involved were too much for her. The power channeled from the sisters' efforts through their place of power in Rose Riley Forest overwhelmed Soriya.

Annabelle had seen her tattoos as a curse for so long. She be-

153

lieved they had marked her as different: a freak of nature unable to connect with those around her. They had driven her from home after home, alone and unwanted. Yet in the end they had saved her from the full force of the ceremony. They had given her the strength to survive.

It was a strength Soriya Greystone now counted on.

Mercy and Mary were too focused on the sphere to care about Annabelle's escape. All they desired was the continuation of their precious ceremony. They depended on its completion for the return of some unknown force that tied them to Portents.

"The power," Mercy said, her eyes aglow with excitement. "It's growing."

"How?" Mary asked.

"The stone," the eldest sister answered. "It was passed down by true acolytes. She is finally fulfilling her destiny."

"Soriya?" Annabelle called. She crept to the edge of the sphere.

Soriya clutched tight to her sides. Her body was covered in small flickers of light. They were pulled from her core, uncontrolled without the proper protection. The stone in her hands glowed with power. A rune was in constant display on the surface, though it shifted with each passing second like a code unlocking the secrets of the door.

"Run," Soriya whispered, the word strained against the pain. "You have to run, Annabelle."

"You'll die," Annabelle replied. "The door—"

"I can..." Soriya stopped. She fought to force the pain down, though Annabelle could see the strain it caused the stone bearer. Soriya let out a series of short breaths to push through the energy coursing from her body. "I can shut it down."

"How?"

"From the inside," she said. "I can do it, Annabelle. I can save Portents."

Mercy came into view, a satisfied grin on her bony face. "A noble sacrifice, Greystone."

Mary arrived from the other side. "It still leaves us our dear sister to use after you're gone."

"Go, Annabelle," Soriya cried before collapsing back to her knees. "Go now!"

Annabelle turned to run. Maggie was waiting and completely cut off all avenues for the overwhelmed woman.

'No way out,' Maggie bellowed in Annabelle's mind. Staples hung from her bleeding lips. *'No way to stop us.'*

The Daughters of Salem closed in on her. They took their time, clearly savoring the terror from the witch at the center of the struggle. This was all Annabelle's fault. This was what all her efforts, all her dreams of finding a purpose, had wrought. The door would bring nothing but darkness just as it always had. She couldn't let that happen. She couldn't let Soriya pay the price for her mistake.

"I don't want to do this... but you've given me no choice," Annabelle said. She jumped at a surprised Maggie with her hands outstretched. The chant upon her lips went unheard, but the result was clear to the other Daughters. Annabelle's hands lit on fire as they grabbed Maggie, transferring the blaze the moment they touched.

Maggie fought to break the connection, but was unsuccessful. *'Her touch! She burns!'*

"What is she doing, Sister?" Mary asked.

'It burns!' Maggie screamed. *'Why? Why does it—'*

Maggie's body turned to ash in Annabelle's grasp. The bone and dust ran through her fingers like grains of sand.

Annabelle's heart pounded. She loomed over the ashes of her fallen sister, abhorred by what she had done. She had spent her life holding back the power inside her, afraid of what it might do to those around her. She could no longer keep it locked inside. Maggie's death had been necessary.

"Betrayer!" Mercy howled.

Mary joined the chorus. "Murderer!"

Both unleashed their magic against the young witch in the green cloak. The force of their mystical energy slammed into Annabelle, yet she did not falter. She stood tall and proud, letting the energy disperse around her.

"What?" Mary said, dropping her hands.

Mercy's eyes widened. "How did you—"

Annabelle turned to face them. She rolled back the sleeves of her cloak to reveal the glowing runes against her skin. The power didn't come from the Daughters' efforts. This time it was through her own means. She had finally accepted her own abilities.

Fire danced in her eyes as she faced her dear sisters. "My turn."

CHAPTER THIRTY-SIX

The battle unfolded before Soriya.

Annabelle took the initial blasts from the Daughters, yet shrugged them off as if they had been meant to tickle her. Mercy and Mary, in their shock, took a step back. Annabelle didn't give them that luxury.

She launched at them with a spell on her lips. Energy crackled at her fingers. Her initial blasts sent the Daughters reeling, and they sought cover in the tree line. With each strike from Annabelle, they were battered farther from the door and their goal.

Soriya could do nothing but watch as the fight continued. Annabelle, however, no longer needed any outside support. The scarlet-haired witch had clearly found her power and confidence during the struggle. Annabelle pressed her attack against the sisters with two streaking bolts of light from her fingertips. Small blazes cropped up in their wake. The Daughters of Salem faltered. They countered what they could by creating shields around their tiring bodies. For the most part, though, they were overpowered by their sister.

And why wouldn't they be overwhelmed by her magic? Annabelle was the doormaker, the one with the potential to give the Daughters what they needed. Everything stemmed from their lost sister, and now they were paying the price for their arrogant demands.

Soriya watched Annabelle fight for her and fight for Portents. Each glimpse came at a cost. Pain ripped through Soriya. The force of the circuit maintaining the bridge to the Bypass threatened to rend her apart. She couldn't feel her legs, and her arms tingled as if on fire.

She tried to push through the pain. Soriya couldn't let Annabelle carry the burden. It was her city at stake. A scream escaped her. A howl ripped from her lungs as she pushed her feet under her. Every inch she gained sent unending waves of electricity through her body; Soriya squeezed the Greystone, hoping its power would bolster her own.

It had become part of the circuit. The runes continued to shift. Vincan to Cyrillac to Gothic and more. The stone was locked in place, working for the Daughters and their goal.

From the other side of the door, shadows began to form. Figures took shape and reached for the threshold. Time was no longer on her side. Soriya needed to break the connection to the Greystone. The circuit had to be interrupted, even if it was only for a moment.

"Soriya…" a distant voice called.

Her eyes flew open. "Who said that?"

She spun in place, searching for the source of the voice. It was not contained in the sphere. It had come from the open door to the Bypass.

"Don't fight this," the voice continued. "Let the door open."

The call boomed through her ears. It was a man's voice, deep and thunderous even against the cacophony around her. Soriya squinted through the swirling mass of light in the open door, unable to make out the shapes still forming within.

"You sound so familiar," she said. The voice calmed and soothed her despite the agony rippling through her battered frame. "Who are you?"

A single shadow took form in the doorway. Hands reached out to her. "You struggle to bring the light, but the dark has its place as well. It shows us the purity of the world. It can free us all. Surrender to it, Soriya."

The voice made sense. Balance had always been her calling. Light and dark worked together to achieve unity for all. She had been a proponent of the strategy ever since Mentor taught it to her. She wanted to listen to more, to hear the voice call her name again. Something about it made her want nothing more than to accept the words as truth and do as she was told.

Do not listen to the voice, my child. He will only lead you astray.

Kok'-Kol had warned her. The black raven had known what was to come and had tried to guide her to the truth, though it wasn't truly needed in this case. If the voice was the true goal of the Daughters of Salem, there was only ever going to be one answer from Soriya.

"I won't," she said.

"You have no choice," the voice replied in anger. Shadowy fists clenched, and the circuit increased. The power pulled from the runes on the stone monoliths burst into a wave of blinding light, and she screamed out in agony.

"No," Soriya said. "There is always a choice."

She shot to her feet and raised the Greystone over her head. Every ounce of will and every spark of defiance ran through her weakened body into the stone. The light dimmed, breaking the display of runes on the surface until only one remained.

Thunder rumbled—building and building—until the first lightning strike shot loose from the clear sky. Bolt after bolt rained down on the clearing. Soriya's screams were lost to the the rending of trees as the Greystone unleashed unbridled destruction all around her.

Annabelle's fight with the Daughters stopped. All turned to witness the display of the Greystone's power. Soriya called forth another barrage, this time toward the stone monoliths. With each strike, the spears cracked and broke. The runes adorning them fell dark.

"No!" Mercy bellowed.

"What has she done?" Mary cried.

The strikes continued. Each slammed to the earth, shattering the peaks of the monoliths. With their runes destroyed, the circuit finally cut out. The sphere surrounding Soriya disappeared.

So did the door. Soriya caught a glimpse of the shadow being pulled back into the Bypass. His hands still reached for his freedom even at the end.

Soriya fell to her knees. The Greystone slipped from her grasp to the ground before her. The Daughters' shadows loomed over her.

"You took it all away from us!" Mercy shouted.

"No," Annabelle called from behind them. The runes on her arms were still lit. "That's my job."

A door formed on the altar. Soriya grabbed the Greystone, then rolled clear of the door before it could fully take shape. The door wasn't like the others. This one had no connection to the Bypass. There was no green energy swirl, nor any link to worlds past, present, and future. There was only a black void.

"You want a door so much, sisters?" Annabelle said. "Here's your damn door."

Wind swept from the Greystone. It pushed the Daughters toward the darkness.

"What are you—" Mary said. She clawed at the air. All sense left her, and she fell into the void.

Mercy made no attempt to save her sister. She dug into the wooden altar, fighting against the gale force generated by the Greystone. "You can't do this to me! We're the same, Annabelle. We're family!"

"Then this shouldn't come as a surprise to you," Annabelle said. "Goodbye, Sister."

Mercy slipped into the darkness. Her howls echoed through the clearing. Soriya lowered the stone. The rune faded so only the clear sheen of the stone remained. Annabelle's arms fell to her sides, and with them the power of her tattoos dimmed.

The void collapsed in on itself, a fitting final sentence for the Daughters of Salem.

CHAPTER THIRTY-SEVEN

Soriya staggered from the altar. Her feet gave way at the edge, and her entire body surrendered to the pain she'd endured. She tipped forward, waiting for the soft grass to welcome her.

Annabelle was there to catch her. The cloaked woman took the brunt of Soriya's weight and kept her from the ground. Shifting Soriya to one side, Annabelle led them away from the small brush fires created during the battle. They passed charred grass left in the wake of the massive door. A safe distance away from the confrontation, Annabelle set Soriya against the base of an intact oak.

Soriya continued to clutch tight to the Greystone. She held it before her until her arm could no longer handle even that simple strain and the stone fell to her side.

"You did it, Annabelle," Soriya said. "You stopped them."

Annabelle collapsed against the base of the tree. She said nothing; her gaze was lost in the destruction before them. Soriya joined her in surveying the devastation. The peaks of the stone monoliths were shattered, and pieces were strewn about the clearing. The altar continued to flicker while the embers of a fire threatened to engulf the entire sacred place with just the right spark.

"It was a beautiful place," Annabelle whispered.

"Annabelle?" Soriya asked. "Are you—"

Annabelle wiped her eyes clear.

"Hey," Soriya said, reaching for her. "It's okay. It's—"

"Was it ever really me?"

Soriya froze. "What?"

"I thought… I thought I needed them," Annabelle said. She leaned her head back against the tree trunk. "My family. I thought I needed a home. The doors I opened, the things I unleashed? Was it ever my choice?"

"I don't understand."

"There was a voice," Annabelle said. "Through the door. Through all the doors. I never realized the voice was there before, not until the Daughters told me about it. Did you hear it when you were… did you hear it?"

She had. Soriya had heard the voice very well indeed, along with the comfort it had brought her. Her skin chilled at the thought, like a forgotten memory was rising to the surface. She had known the voice somehow. She had recognized the tone and the inflection, as if it had been ingrained in her very being.

"I…" Soriya didn't know what to say that Annabelle might understand. The experience had frightened the stone bearer—the idea that someone waited on the other side of the veil for release. It frightened her to think they had the power to influence the actions of others in the world. How could she not have known such a thing was possible? How could Mentor not have known?

"It's over, Annabelle," Soriya said, attempting to reassure the woman. There was no reason to upset Annabelle further. "Whatever it was, whatever the Daughters said to you, they can't hurt you again. They can't make you do anything."

Annabelle jumped to her feet. Her fists clenched in frustration as she paced before an exhausted Soriya. "You're wrong," she snapped. Watery eyes widened. "You are!"

"Annabelle—"

"You weren't there," she continued, unable to hold back the tears and the anger. "For a moment, for a single second, I was willing to do *anything* for them. If it meant having a family, I would have done anything to make it happen."

"But you didn't," Soriya replied.

"I wanted to!" Annabelle shouted. "And then? When you took my place? I almost left you. I almost ran away, like I always do."

"Annabelle, listen to me," Soriya said. "You were scared. So was I! But you didn't run. You didn't give in. You stood up and fought back. You saved us. You saved Portents."

"No," Annabelle said, shoulders slumped and head bowed. "That wasn't me. That was you."

Annabelle turned away from Soriya. She rounded the stone monoliths, her hand grazing the once beautiful artifacts from a lifetime ago. The stone bearer's concern grew with each step the scarlet-haired witch took. She couldn't let Annabelle leave, not after everything they had been through, and especially not on her own.

"Where are you going, Annabelle?" Soriya called. "You can't just walk away."

Annabelle stopped at the edge of the clearing and turned back. There was sadness in her eyes. "I have to."

"You still don't know what—"

"I won't… There won't be any more doors," she said over Soriya's plea. "There won't. I can promise you that. I can't stay here, though. Not after what they told me, and not after what I learned about my… what might have been my ancestor."

"That's not you, Annabelle," Soriya said. "You can see that, can't you?"

Annabelle nodded slightly. "I can."

"Then stay."

"I wish… I wish I had your strength, Soriya," Annabelle said. "I wish I had your courage to keep going."

"You do," Soriya answered without question. "I've seen it."

"Maybe someday," Annabelle said. She lifted the hood of her cloak over her head and dropped her weary eyes into shadow. "But not today."

"Annabelle!" Soriya yelled after her. It failed to stop the scared woman from leaving. Her steps were quick, and she faded into the thick brush.

Soriya tried to stand and follow, but the effort fell short.

"Annabelle, wait…"

Soriya slipped from the side of the tree and crashed to the ground. The exhaustion had finally caught up with her. Her battered body could do no more for her, so Soriya closed her eyes for some much-needed sleep.

CHAPTER THIRTY-EIGHT

Sunlight shone from above by the time Mentor found her. He had spent hours searching. His knee ached as he trudged deeper into the woods of Rose Riley Park. Every instinct told him to rest—even for only a minute—but he resisted the temptation. He needed to find Soriya.

After Mentor had watched the spell depart the city, those that had been afflicted and were still conscious had been disoriented. No one had remembered the change, nor did they recall their activities while turned. Mentor and Urg had worked with those lost and confused to get them to a safe shelter as dawn broke over the city. Once there, they had been able to contact family members and loved ones in order to retrieve them. The night had ended with a whimper, not the bang Mentor had imagined.

No, that part had fallen to Soriya.

With the witches' victims intact and safe, Mentor had turned his attention to his student's whereabouts. Urg, concerned as well, had wanted to join him. Mentor, though, had noted the orc's exhaustion and promised to call after it was over.

Mentor had followed the trail for miles, winding through city streets until reaching the edge of the forest. By the time he had made it there, the eerie light from the spell was gone. Still, Mentor had pressed ahead and pushed through his pain to make the upward climb into the woods. He had circled the embankment half a dozen times before he'd found tracks on the ground.

It had taken him hours to reach the clearing. Mentor stepped out from the thick brush and nearly stumbled from the uneven earth. He was too busy looking around the space, at the altar and the stone monoliths rounding the back half. He had never seen such a place, not in all his years of study.

"Incredible," he muttered in astonishment.

The stone monoliths were broken, shattered by an extreme force. Charred edges marred the altar. Trees lay along the outskirts, both on the ground and leaning on their neighbors. The earth groaned with each shift, like it had yet to settle from the cataclysmic battle.

Mentor found Soriya lying beside the trunk of a nearby oak. Cuts lined her body, and dried blood had mixed with a layer of mud on her skin.

"Soriya," he called.

The sound was enough to stir her from her slumber. She rolled to her side, pushing the hair from her face as she woke. Every shift was a struggle; the pain caused her to visibly wince. Mentor helped her find some support against the side of the tree.

"Hey," she said. It was so casual, Mentor couldn't help but laugh.

"Hey yourself," he replied. "This place—"

"It used to look a lot nicer," she said. The stone was in her hand. He took it from her and cradled it close. The Greystone cooled his skin, yet even through his palm he could feel the energy still flowing from the enigmatic weapon.

Mentor grabbed the tree and lowered to the ground at her side before returning the stone. "Are you okay?"

"I'm fine." She wiped her eyes and gave a loud yawn. "I just needed a few minutes to rest. What time is it?"

"Late morning," Mentor said.

"Okay. I guess I needed a few *hours*, then." Shaking away her extended nap, Soriya turned to him. Concern filled her as she noted his tattered robes and bloodied knuckles. "Hey, are you all—?"

He waved the question down. "Just a long night. Nothing more."

"Tell me about it."

Soriya leaned back and put all her weight on the tree. Mentor joined her. Each took a deep breath, filling their lungs with the fresh air. The chirping of birds rang out from above. The sound of the woods became more and more alive in the silence of their thoughts.

"It's peaceful here," Mentor said. "I don't usually get out this way."

Soriya chuckled. "Nothing like an attack from some pissed-off witches to make you appreciate the beauty of nature."

Mentor nodded. "Sun feels good, too."

"Not going to argue with…" Soriya cut herself off. She reached into her back pocket and pulled out her cell phone. It continued to buzz for a brief moment before Soriya answered it. "Hello?"

She held the phone tighter to her ear, trying to listen. Then she pulled the device away.

"Is something wrong?"

"It was Beth," she said. "I think. The call dropped out. No signal out here, I guess."

The phone buzzed once more. Beth had left a message.

"We should go," Mentor said. "You can call her back."

"I'm sure it can wait," she said. Tired eyes scanned the display before Soriya tucked the device away. She stretched her arms out and gave another yawn. "I can't believe it's late morning."

Soriya slowly worked her way to her feet. Moving from the shadow of the tree, she stepped into the light to let the sun wash over her. A smile crested upon her lips as she soaked up the bright rays.

Suddenly, her eyes shot wide open. Mentor could see the realization set in even before the words left her.

"Wait," she said. "Late morning?"

Mentor laughed. "I was wondering if you would figure it out."

"I did it?"

"You did."

She had passed the final test. Soriya jumped into the air, kicking her legs out as she hollered into the open sky, "I did it!"

Mentor joined her in the light. "That and more, little one.

You stood up to the darkness. You saved a lot of lives last night, and you did it all on your own."

The celebrating ended. Soriya's gaze drifted away toward the woods. When she came back to him, Soriya took him by the hands and squeezed.

"No," she said. "Never on my own."

"You passed this final test, Soriya," Mentor said. "A gauntlet of a night, to be sure. I am proud to call you Greystone."

"Greystone," she breathed with a smile on her face.

"It's yours now."

They turned from the clearing and headed back down the path. Through the shattered tree line, Portents stretched out for as far as they could see. The city sparkled in the sunlight, pristine in her glory. The job was Soriya's now, fully and completely. There would always be more lessons to learn, but they would do it as equals.

"And everything that comes with it."

Soriya was the Greystone now. She was the protector of every home and every life in the city of Portents. Mentor knew without a doubt she would honor the job. She would always make him proud.

CHAPTER THIRTY-NINE

Eddie hesitated at the door. His hand hovered over the frame, unable to commit. His other hand held tight to the strap of Sherry's purse.

He had found it in the aftermath. First, he'd had to get rid of his unwanted guests. They had been quick to stir once they'd recovered. Startled by the state of their ragged clothes, the two men had exchanged curious looks with each other. No words had been spoken, and none were needed. The two men had departed immediately, clearly hoping to avoid the awkward stares of the waking city.

Eddie had been glad for the solitude, though once he'd glanced around at the devastation left by their visit, part of him wished the two men would have at least volunteered to help clean up. Resigning himself to the task, Eddie had set to work, sweeping up the majority of the glass. He had also shifted the debris from his shattered projects to one corner of the store to give him better access to the street and the back room.

Parched and starved from the long night, Eddie had retired to his workshop. He'd found the purse resting on his desk. Sherry had forgotten it in her hurry to get home. *To get away from me*, Eddie had thought before slapping some sense into his addled brain. She had been worried about her mother, nothing more. There had been no reason to add more to her explanation, yet it took all his willpower not to let his imagination run wild with theories.

He hadn't wanted to rummage through Sherry's belongings to find her address. The debate had raged for almost fifteen minutes before he'd been able to justify the simple act of finding her license. How could he not return it after everything?

It was that question that finally pushed him to knock on the apartment door. Three quick raps announced his presence. A shadow ran under the frame. Shuffling feet and mumbled curses moved closer to the door. The sliding of the chain and the clicking of locks preceded the opening of the door. A middle-aged woman wearing a bathrobe greeted him. A cigarette dangled precariously from her lips, and ash sprinkled down the front of her with each subtle shift.

"Yeah?" she said in a raspy voice.

"Uh, hello," Eddie said. He waved awkwardly, unable to find the words. He'd expected Sherry to answer.

"You here to fix the cable?"

The living room stretched behind her. There was a television in the corner, and the screen flickered and faded with different static patterns. There were two full-size couches positioned in the middle of the room in the shape of an L. A rocking chair rested between them, though it seemed to serve as a table more than a place to sit.

"No, I—"

She started to close the door, disinterested. "Don't want any. Already have them. I'm happy with my cell phone provider. I don't vote. Whatever the pitch, I'm good."

"Wait," Eddie said. His hand slammed against the door to keep it open. "I…"

"I already heard the *I* from you," the woman remarked. She took a long drag from her cigarette and blew the smoke at him. "And what's with the purse?"

"Huh?" Eddie asked as he wafted the cloud from his face. He lifted the purse, barely recalling its presence. "Oh yeah. I found it. That's all."

"Good for you," she replied. "Goes with the outfit."

Eddie shook his head. "It's not mine."

"Are you sure?"

"Yes," he snapped. He took a sharp breath to calm his nerves. "Look. It's Sherry's purse. She lives here, right?"

A silent stare was all the answer he received.

Sweat dotted Eddie's brow. "Please tell me she lives here because I don't know if I can do this again. Couldn't be worse than this, though, right?" Her eyes thinned, and panic set in for Eddie. "Not that you're the worst, but… Okay. Sherry left this at my shop last night, so I thought—"

"Eddie?" a voice called from behind the woman in the bathrobe.

Sherry stood in the shallow hallway of the apartment. She dabbed at her soaked hair with a towel. A tight t-shirt and jeans combo made Eddie's heart beat faster.

"You know this hooligan?" the woman asked.

"Eddie!" Sherry exclaimed. She dropped the towel and ran for the door. The older woman shifted aside before being knocked away from the excited young lady. Sherry jumped at Eddie, wrapping her arms around him and kissing him.

"Sherry Ginger Dolan!" the woman cried. "What are you doing?"

Sherry ended the kiss and settled next to Eddie. He could feel the heat radiating off her. It soothed his exhausted body.

She beamed at him. "He saved my life last night, Ma. I told you."

"Him?" Her mother balked. Both threw her a glare. "He did? *This* is Eddie?"

Eddie cleared his throat and extended his hand. "Edward Smith, ma'am. Nice to meet you."

The woman took a drag from her cigarette and stared at him. It was the way everyone looked at him at first. The look made him feel like he was nothing more than a worthless little thief for the Domingo family, and that he would never be anything more.

He knew better now. He *had* changed. Last night had been proof, not that any had ever been required. All he'd needed was the confidence to recognize the change.

He continued to hold out his hand. Sherry sighed. "Ma…"

The woman stamped out her cigarette in a nearby ashtray. When she returned, her look softened and a slight smile settled on her lips. She took his hand.

"Thank you."

"Right time, right place," Eddie said.

"For me especially." Sherry hugged him tighter.

Sherry's mother waved him inside. "There's coffee in the pot. How do you like your eggs?"

"I don't really—" He paused. Sherry pushed him deeper into the apartment, then closed the door. She took his hand in hers and squeezed. Her mother started for the kitchen. "However you prefer them is fine, ma'am."

She nodded before exiting the room. Eddie and Sherry stood alone. The static of the television provided background noise to their shared silence. They smiled to each other, shifting closer and closer together. Sherry rose up on her toes and kissed him once more.

"I'm glad you came," she said.

Eddie's grin widened, truly happy for the first time in a long time. He had been worried he'd never feel anything but perpetual guilt over the mistakes of the past, but the truth was that *he* was the one holding himself back. He had refused to accept the change he'd undergone since leaving behind the Domingo family in both spirit and name.

His life was different now. It was better than it had ever been, and he couldn't wait to see what happened next.

"Me too," Eddie said as the pair headed for the kitchen. "Me too."

CHAPTER FORTY

The fries were delicious. They were coated with cheddar cheese and sliced-up bacon, and Soriya shoveled down wave after wave. Moans of satisfaction escaped her with each bite, loud enough that she drew curious stares from the rest of the diner.

Urg could do nothing to quiet her. With each stray glance from the other patrons, he retreated farther and farther into the booth. He kept the brim of his black fedora low to hide his features.

After finishing the plate, Soriya licked her fingers of the strands of cheese that attempted to escape her endless appetite. The dish joined four others on the table. All sat in front of her with only a small cup of tea resting before her companion, who looked on with awe.

"Where do you put it all?"

"Don't judge me. I earned this."

Urg smiled. "That you did."

The waiter passed by. Seeing the empty dishes spread across the table, he reached into his apron pouch and retrieved a piece of paper. Urg snatched the check from his hand before the waiter could set it on the table. The kid's eyes grew panicked at the sight of Urg's green skin and the spikes at his wrist. He walked away quickly and almost collided into a pair of departing guests as he stared back at the orc.

"Urg." Soriya held out her hand. "You don't have to pay."

"I feel bad about leaving Mentor the way I did," Urg replied. "I should have helped look for you."

"It's okay," she said. "You had people to check on, too."

"And a nap to take," Urg said with a grimace. Soriya could see how much the fight had taken out of him in his slumped frame and the cuts that marred his usually impervious hide.

"Let me pay."

"Consider it your graduation gift." Urg scanned the tally on the long receipt. His eyes grew wider the farther he made it down the slip. They darted between the receipt and the empty dishes. "And your Christmas present, it seems."

"Urg…"

He pointed at the bill. "When did you order a cheeseburger?"

"When you were in the bathroom." Soriya sighed. She patted her gut as she settled against the cushion of the booth. "Give me the check."

"Forget it," Urg said. He pulled out his wallet.

"Urg, come on. I can—"

"Don't fight me on this, Soriya." He placed the bill at the end of the table with his credit card on top. The waiter circled back seconds later to retrieve the payment. He took the card without a word, though he had the same terrified look on his face.

"I won't fight you," Soriya said. A smile grew on her lips. "Wouldn't want to mess up your suit any more than it is." She pointed to the white stain running down his shoulder. She would have given anything to have seen his face after the bird let loose on him. "Want to tell me what happened?"

"*Nothing* happened," Urg snapped. A groan escaped him. He tried to wipe it clean with a wet napkin. It did little but spread the mess. He tossed the napkin to the table in frustration, then crossed his arms. "Shut up."

"I hear it's good luck," Soriya said, holding back a laugh.

"Then the bird can pay my dry-cleaning bill," Urg replied. The waiter returned with Urg's credit card and two copies of the check. Urg signed one, then pocketed the other with his card. He dropped a twenty on the table for a tip as he stood. "Come on."

Soriya joined him in the aisle. He walked away quickly, and Soriya tried to keep up, but the sound of the television positioned over the counter at the front of the establishment drew her attention.

"… where investigators found the body of a young woman," the reporter continued. "She has yet to be identified, but sources at the Central Precinct confirmed that she is the latest to be attributed to the Kindly Killer—the name given to the monster who has already left four dead, all with smiles on their faces."

There was a killer among them. It was the first Soriya had heard about the series of deaths. It was another menace on the loose and another job that required her attention.

"Soriya?" Urg called from the door.

"Yeah," she said as she turned away from the newscast. "I'm coming."

Outside, the sun was in decline. A warm front brought with it higher-than-normal temperatures and the illusion of another week of summer before autumn finally took hold. Pedestrians walked the block, men in shorts and women in dresses. They roamed the shops and the restaurants to fill their day before the sun disappeared.

Little had been reported on the previous night. Loud disturbances and unruly behavior had made the papers, but there was nothing about the dark reflections unleashed by the witches' spell. The entire event had been covered up, hidden from the public. Those who had been there remembered, though. They likely would for the rest of their lives.

Soriya caught up with Urg at the sidewalk. The pair traveled north along the quiet strip of businesses toward downtown. "You working tonight?"

"In a couple hours," Urg said with a nod. He rolled his eyes at the sight of the stain on his shoulder. "Plenty of time to change. Though at this point I might have to wear sweatpants and a t-shirt."

"I always said you should show off your spikes more."

A group of teens passed by. Their stares and wide, gaping mouths caused Urg to grumble under his breath. He lowered the brim of his hat more to hide his skin tone.

"Maybe I can find a turtleneck or something."

Soriya started to laugh, then stopped. All forward momentum slowed to a grinding halt, which caused Urg's shoes to squeal along the sidewalk.

"Soriya?"

She stood in front of the boarded-up window of the Wiccan shop. A few shards of shattered glass decorated the sidewalk. Soriya kicked at them, unable to shake her responsibility in the damage done. The wood covering the shop was decorated with spray paint. Large black letters read OUT OF BUSINESS for all to see.

Soriya shifted to the front door for a better look. The destruction she'd caused to the back half of the building dominated the view, yet more had been done in the aftermath thanks to the Daughters of Salem. Shelves were knocked down, the contents smashed and broken. There was nothing left to save for Annabelle.

Soriya had hoped to see her inside. She'd wanted another chance to change the woman's mind after their last conversation. More than that, Soriya wanted Annabelle to stay in Portents, or hoped at the very least that the scarlet-haired witch had found the strength to *want* to stay.

"She was just looking for a home," Soriya said as Urg joined her at the shop. "Now she's lost this one, too."

"Any idea where she might have gone?" he asked. "Who she might turn to?"

"None."

He patted her shoulder. "Give her time. She may reach out, find some way to contact you."

"Contact?" The word hit her like a ton of bricks. Her eyes widened. "My phone."

She reached for her back pocket and pulled out the small device. The notification was still there. She had completely forgotten about Beth's call. She had been so wrapped up in the news of her success at her final test she'd failed to actually listen to the message. She entered her code at the prompt and waited for the voicemail to play.

Beth's voice filled the speaker. "Soriya. I need your help."

Soriya nearly dropped the phone. She had never heard such fear from her friend.

"What is it?" Urg asked. "Soriya?"

The phone silenced. She lowered it to her side. "I have to go."

She tucked the device away, then turned to leave. She barely heard Urg over the pounding of her heart in her chest. "Of course you do."

She stopped. After running back to him, Soriya gave him a peck on the cheek. "You're the best, Urg. Thanks for everything."

"Congrats, kid."

Soriya nodded before running off down the streets of Portents for the Knoll. All sense of joy at passing her final test left her. Her friend needed her.

Only Beth mattered now.

CHAPTER FORTY-ONE

Urg couldn't help but smile at Soriya's quick departure. There was such a persistence in her, an unwavering strength that allowed her to carry on even after last night's ordeal.

He certainly felt whipped from the affair. His body ached, and every muscle screamed from his head to his toes for a massage. The temptation continued to creep up to check on his protrusions, to make sure his spikes were back to normal, and to see if his teeth had shrunk to their usual size.

Yet there was Soriya. She headed off to face her next challenge as if nothing had happened. *And she wondered how the world was so quick to move on.* She was the poster child for change, always growing and moving ahead, despite the pain that seemed to dog her past.

She reminded him why he stayed in the city, why he continued to work in the community and surround himself with the people of Portents. In their own little way, they needed each other. From a smile on the subway to a greeting at the grocery store, there was a reason for them to be part of the community. They were each a piece of the whole.

Somehow Urg knew that Soriya stood at the center of it all. She held them all together and propped them all up through sheer force of will. Her spirit was undeniable. It had sure as hell saved his life the night before. Just the memory of Soriya had kept him from eviscerating Rachel on the street. She brought him back, pulled him from the depths of the witches' spell and gave him a chance to make things right. It hadn't been through her words or her actions, but with her spirit. Her friendship had saved him.

Urg's grin carried him down the block. Work would come quick, but there was still time to enjoy the sunset and the life that seemed to envelop the city around him.

He did, of course, need a change of clothes first. However, even the bird shit on his shoulder couldn't dampen the light-hearted nature of his stroll or the carefree attitude he passed along to others as they walked by.

He hoped it would last. Not only for himself but for Soriya, who had worked so hard to achieve her goal of being the Grey-stone. She'd earned the role and continued to each and every day. He was proud to know her and even prouder to stand by her side when she called.

Soriya was the real reason he stayed, his real purpose when it came to Portents. She was the light for those in need. She stood against the darkness, and she did it without pomp and pageant-ry. Her only desire was to make a difference.

Urg could do no less. Her challenges had just begun, and he would help see her through them. He would be at her side... until the very end.

CHAPTER FORTY-TWO

She should have listened to the message right away. That one thought circled on Soriya as she raced across the city for King's Lane at the heart of the Knoll. The phone had been given for a specific reason, but when the time came, Soriya had missed the call. Soriya had ignored the only cry for help Bethany Loren probably ever sent in her life.

Beth's voice echoed in Soriya's mind. There was fear behind her words. What the hell had been so important that Soriya hadn't called her back?

Soriya slipped through the unlocked kitchen window overlooking the fire escape at the rear of the property. Her feet crept along the floorboards to minimize the creaking of the wood. She didn't know who or what to expect at such a strange hour.

The apartment sat in darkness. The low sun in the distance cast a shadow through the space. Soriya heard no movement. No one shifted around in the bedrooms down the hall or the living room adjacent to her. She continued forward, inch by inch, her concern both ebbing and rising as she stepped deeper into the home.

Nothing had changed since her last visit. Everything about Beth was stable and rock-solid. That had always brought a certain degree of comfort to Soriya: Beth would always be there for her no matter what.

When Soriya reached the window and peered outside, she learned the truth. Sirens echoed in the distance. They appeared unable to circumvent the traffic along the Knoll. No cars moved. They were all locked in place as their occupants stared at the crowd congregating along the sidewalk in front of the apartment building.

At the center of the gathering was Beth.

Her husband Greg knelt at her side, tears running from his eyes. The bystanders surrounding them said little, but their murmurs filled the air. Soriya could not hear Beth's whispers to her husband over the noise.

She could not hear her friend's final words.

All Soriya saw was the woman's smile. It was the same as it had always been: so bright and assured. Her resilience had always inspired Soriya and had always pushed her to do more and be more than she'd thought possible. Now it was the last thing Beth offered before her eyes closed to the world. Then she was gone.

"No."

Soriya stepped back from the window. Her hand covered her quivering lips. Her legs felt unsteady, and she fell to her knees. Outside, lights flashed brighter. Police took photographs of the scene as officers attempted to disperse the crowd surrounding Beth.

I wasn't there for her. How could I not have been there for her? Soriya's failure screamed for an answer, but none came. Instead, the only thing running through her mind were Beth words from a month earlier.

"You might think of this as the end, as your last challenge to become the Greystone. But it's really only the start for you. Your world is going to get so much bigger, and with that comes change. It happens to everyone. The world moves on."

Beth had been right. There was no final gauntlet, nor any final test of Soriya's skills. There was only the end of one challenge and the start of the next.

Soriya had been stupid to believe life would stand still for her while she grew and progressed—that everything would always stay the same. That comfort she'd needed had been the ideal of a child. Soriya should have known better.

Wiping the tears from her eyes, Soriya made her way back to her feet. She held tight to the wall for support as she returned to the window and the world outside.

The crowd had all but dispersed. Greg Loren, however, remained at his wife's side. He held her hand, sobbing over Beth's broken body. No one reached for him, and no one offered him any solace. They gave him nothing, not even a kind word or a shoulder to cry on. The world left him to his grief alone.

Soriya couldn't let that happen. Not after her mistake with the missed call. Beth had deserved better from her friend. Soriya should have been at her side to fight whatever it was that had been after her—the danger that had worried her last month when they'd met over breakfast.

Greg Loren deserved the same. Beth had loved him with all her heart and cherished every moment they had shared together. Everything she had ever done was for him so he could thrive in the city that wasn't his own.

"I'll help him, Beth," she pledged in the solitude of the apartment. "I'll be there for him. I promise."

It was all she could think of to make up for her error. It was in her promise that Soriya found the strength to keep going rather than crumble to the floor in despair and hopelessness.

Beth was dead.

But Greg was still alive. He needed her... even if he didn't know it yet.

Soriya started to leave. Her hurried steps were uneven, and she accidentally bumped against the coffee table in the living room. Loose pieces of paper tumbled from the piles strewn across the small wooden surface and scattered on the ground. As Soriya picked them up, she thumbed through each in turn.

All related to the Kindly Killer. They were in Greg's handwriting, including his notes and thoughts on the case. Greg had been actively tracking the monster.

Soriya put back the personal notes. She carefully laid them on the disparate piles accumulating on the coffee table. Then she pawed through the case reports. Grabbing a pen tucked between files, Soriya jotted down several notes gleaned from her reading.

As Soriya left, her eyes still stinging from the held back tears, she suddenly knew exactly how to help Detective Greg Loren.

CHAPTER FORTY-THREE

Annabelle Waterhouse stood at the edge of the forest. She stared out at Portents in the fading light of day. Her hand grazed the bark of a tall oak at her side. Her fingers dug into the wood for support. The city was so far away yet still so close to her.

She had tried to leave. When she'd left Soriya in the woods, Annabelle had had a firm plan in mind. Leaving Portents had been the only thing occupying her troubled thoughts. So much of what had happened had been her fault. She couldn't risk it occurring again—even inadvertently. She'd closed her shop; the damage had been too extensive to salvage anything in the wreckage. All her collections and all her work from the last few years had been destroyed in a single night. From there she had made her way home to pack a bag. Just one, with some essentials: clothes, her toothbrush, and a notebook to catalog her thoughts.

The bag sat beside her feet at the edge of the forest. She turned to face the city one last time.

In the end, she hadn't been able to leave. It felt like a betrayal to everything she had gone through. It felt like turning her back on a fight that hadn't truly ended. For Annabelle, it felt like the fight had just begun.

However, she couldn't stay in her apartment. Nor could she return to the shop that had consumed so much of her time for the last few years. She had opened it for selfish reasons while pretending to care about the needs of others—but truthfully the needs were her own. She'd used the store to find the books, the research materials, and the spellwork necessary to track down her answers. Now that she had found her answers, she wished she had never sought them out in the first place.

If Annabelle stayed and pretended her life was the same as it had been only thirty-six hours earlier, it would have been a lie. There would have also been a price to pay for such a lie. She would find herself exploited once more, placed in danger for the sake of powers she still did not completely understand. The doors were hers to control, and taking herself off the board was the only way to ensure they remained closed for everyone's sake.

The forest called to her. Annabelle sensed the call emanating from deep within the confines of Rose Riley Forest. It had started with a dull hum, like a song caught on the wind or playing behind the closed windows of a passing car. The sound drew her away from the commotion of downtown to the quiet peace of the woods that occupied her border.

Annabelle finished her look back at the city. A small tear sat in her eye. It was a remembrance of the few good days she would always keep locked in her memory. To deny that there had been happy memories would have been foolish, and she offered a silent promise to never let them fade. She swiped the tear away, letting it run down her finger to the grass beneath her feet.

Annabelle slung her bag over her shoulder. She stepped out of view of the city and headed deeper into the woods. She followed the thin path through the brush. The trail led her uphill. It wound across miles of landscape until she reached the clearing and the remnants of the seven monoliths that had once decorated the sacred space.

Beyond the semi-circle, Annabelle pushed aside overgrown brush. Tree limbs snapped from the efforts and crunched under her feet. Once she had cleared them away, she found a path that cut through the woods.

Curious steps carried her along the path. Darkness followed her as the sun continued to set in the distance. At the end of the trail, behind a wall of downed tree branches and shattered trunks, Annabelle found the source of the call.

There, set against the side of the cliff that doubled as the border of Portents, was a home. The second the dilapidated structure came into view, the siren song that had drawn her from the city grew quiet. She knew who it had belonged to as soon as she saw it. The home had been built by the Daughters of Salem. The modest domicile had been their sanctuary. Now, it was hers.

They were still connected, even after everything she had done to them. She was one of them, though she fought the familial ties with every fiber of her being.

Annabelle reached for the crooked door to the ramshackle cottage. Wood creaked under her heels, and she found herself gazing back toward the city once more.

Part of her hoped to return. Another part of her knew that someday she would. She knew on some level she would see Soriya and help when the time came—when the darkness finally and inevitably took hold.

Annabelle entered the home of her sisters to bide her time for when she would be needed once again.

ABOUT THE AUTHOR

Lou Paduano is the author of the Greystone series of urban fantasy adventures, which follow Detective Greg Loren and Soriya Greystone as they hunt myths, monsters, and legends in the city of Portents.

He is also the author of the conspiracy thriller series, The DSA, a serialized tale about a clandestine government agency trying to discover the true power behind humanity's future.

He lives in Grand Island, New York with his wife and three daughters. Sign up for his e-mail list for free content as well as updates on future releases at loupaduano.com.

THE GREYSTONE SAGA

AVAILABLE NOW

Follow the adventures of Soriya Greystone and Detective Greg Loren as they hunt dangerous myths and legends in the city of Portents.

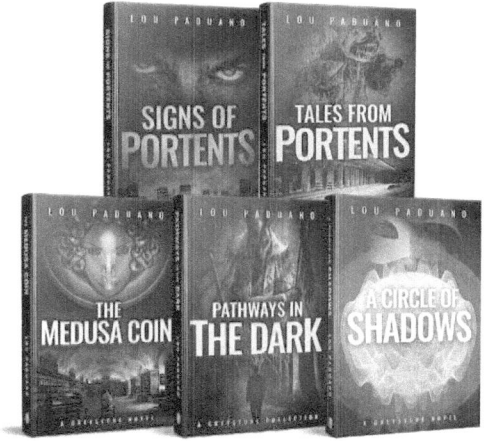

BOOK ONE - SIGNS OF PORTENTS
BOOK TWO - TALES FROM PORTENTS
BOOK THREE - THE MEDUSA COIN
BOOK FOUR - PATHWAYS IN THE DARK
BOOK FIVE - A CIRCLE OF SHADOWS

GREYSTONE-IN-TRAINING

AVAILABLE NOW

For years, Soriya trained to become the Greystone.
Follow the trials that made her the protector
Portents needed to fend off the darkest of threats.

BOOK ONE - HAMMER AND ANVIL
BOOK TWO - THE GIFTS OF KALI
BOOK THREE - THE FINAL GAUNTLET

THE DSA SEASON ONE
AVAILABLE NOW

Ben Riley is recruited into a secret government organization and finds himself knee-deep in a mystery that will change the world...

BOOK ONE - THE CLEARING
BOOK TWO - PROMETHEAN
BOOK THREE - THE BRIDGE
BOOK FOUR - SPECTRAL ADVOCATE
BOOK FIVE - DARK IMPULSES
BOOK SIX - BROKEN LOYALTIES

GREYSTONE CONTINUES IN…

The Kindly Killer stalks the streets of Portents…

Seven victims have been claimed by the murderous madman. No connections exist between the deceased. No clues remain at the scenes.

Greg Loren knows the killer is behind the death of his wife and he's willing to do anything to prove it. Crossing lines comes at a cost, though, both personally and professionally.

Soriya Greystone watches him from a distance, afraid to pull him into her world. But when the twin masked menaces of Comedy and Tragedy strike the city with a chaotic crime wave, the pair are forced together.

How are these two disparate threats connected? And what is the secret behind the Kindly Killer's mania?